o'r stoc

# MR. BUDD INVESTIGATES

The canvas, seemingly daubs of red and green paint, showed, on closer inspection, a woman, her crimson lips twisted in a devilish leer . . . The man who had purchased the painting was found in his lodgings — stabbed to death — his painting stolen. While investigating the case, Superintendent Budd stumbles onto another murder in progress in a derelict house, and hears the dying man utter just two words: 'Red . . . light . . . ' Nearby, lies a picture . . . of the Leering Lady.

GERALD VERNER

# MR. BUDD
# INVESTIGATES

Complete and Unabridged

# LINFORD
*Leicester*

First published in Great Britain

First Linford Edition
published 2013

British Library CIP Data

Verner, Gerald.
  Mr. Budd investigates. - -
(Linford mystery library)
  1. Budd, Robert (Fictitious character)- -
Fiction. 2. Detective and mystery stories.
  3. Large type books.
  I. Title II. Series
  823.9′12–dc23

  ISBN 978–1–4448–1403–3

Published by
F. A. Thorpe (Publishing)
Anstey, Leicestershire

Set by Words & Graphics Ltd.
Anstey, Leicestershire
Printed and bound in Great Britain by
T. J. International Ltd., Padstow, Cornwall

This book is printed on acid-free paper

# 1

# The Leering Lady

# 1

## The Picture

Christmas was very near.

Its proximity was evident in the gaily decorated shop windows with their coloured lights and cotton-wool snow and the chains of artificial holly, whose green leaves and berries were greener and redder than ever appeared in Nature. It was evident in the rows of plump turkeys hanging from the shining steel rails outside the butchers' and the poulterers'; smooth, comfortable-looking birds, that reminded one of prosperous old gentlemen who had retired from business. It was evident in the huge piles of oranges and rosy-faced apples outside the greengrocers' and fruiterers'. It was evident in the excited faces and suppressed eagerness of the children, and in the white mantle of snow, which Nature, having apparently made up her mind for once to do the thing properly, had spread over the land.

In London, the busy streets were thronged with shoppers, not quite so busy as they would be later in the last desperate rush for forgotten presents, but quite busy enough with a crowd of laughing, jostling, eager people, who minded none the least the mud which was all that was left of the snow that had fallen overnight. In London, on this twenty-first day of December, Big Ben boomed out the hour of twelve as it had done for countless other days, but with what seemed an added heartiness, as though it, too, were responding to the spirit of Yuletide. And in Midchester, a hundred and forty miles away, the town hall clock, a distant echo, followed suit exactly three and a half minutes later.

Mr. Budd, that stout and lethargic man, drained the contents of his tankard, wished the genial landlord of the Crown and Anchor good day, and went ponderously off to take his leave of Inspector Haslett, preparatory to catching the three-forty-five train to London from Midchester Junction. His business in Midchester was completed, and he was looking forward to a few days quiet holiday in his little Streatham villa. On his way to the police station he passed the closed and shuttered Theatre Royal without giving it a thought, for he never imagined that behind that rather gloomy exterior with its glaring posters announcing the forthcoming production of Messrs. Harvey and MacLellon's 'Grand Spectacular Pantomime, *Beauty and the Beast*', was at that moment beginning the first incident in a mystery that was to force him to change his plans about catching the London train and spend his Christmas in Midchester . . .

Mr. Oswald Hope, the producer of the pantomime, was conducting a rehearsal. He was a small, rather stout man, whose fat interfered with his breathing and caused him to speak throatily and huskily. He was sitting in the third row of the sheeted stalls, watching the last scene with critical eyes.

'That's right!' he wheezed, his small, beady eyes darting in all directions. 'That's right! Keep it up, and make it snappy. What's that girl doing there? What's she think she is, eh? Hi! Just a moment!'

He clapped his chubby hands and hoisted himself to a standing position.

'You there — third from the right — What's-yer-name? Lily! You're not playing the sleeping beauty in this show, yer know!'

Lily, a slim girl, with hair the colour of well-polished brass, reddened.

'What's the matter, Mr. Hope?' she lisped.

'You weren't kickin'. Your leg was a good foot below all the others!' shouted Mr. Hope. 'Now, let's have it again, and let it go with a swing. All right, Jack' — he nodded to the pianist — 'from the beginning of that last chorus. Now — one — two — three — right!'

Principals and chorus took up the strains of the finale as the pianist thumped it out — this was the sixth time they had been through it that morning — and Mr. Hope watched and listened. The last crashing bars echoed through the empty auditorium, and he nodded.

'That's better,' he announced crisply. 'It's not right, but it's better. I want that converging line to be a line. Get that? At the present moment it sags in the middle. Now we'll get back to the beginning — '

'Excuse me, Mr. Hope — ' The stage manager appeared from the gloom of the wings.

'Well, what is it?' snapped Mr. Hope.

'What about those dresses?' asked the stage manager, leaning forward over the footlights.

'What dresses?' demanded Mr. Hope irritably.

'The dresses for the colour-change scene,' explained the stage manager. 'Mrs. Dickson wants the girls to try them on — in case there should be any alteration.'

'Oh, yes.' Mr. Hope nodded his partially bald head. 'Glad you reminded me, Fred. I'd forgotten all about it. You girls, go along up to the wardrobe.' He looked at his watch. 'The rest of you can break for lunch. We'll start again at two — sharp.'

'Mr. Hope!' the girl who was playing Beauty called softly, as he was turning away towards the pass-door.

'All right, my dear, I'm coming up.' He made for the exit, and a small, narrow iron door that led up to the stage. Passing through, he emerged from the prompt corner and crossed the stage towards her. 'What is it?' he asked.

'Do you mind if I'm a little late in getting back?' she said. 'I've got to go and see about my shoes.'

'No; that's all right,' said Mr. Hope. 'Where are you getting 'em — Robertson's?'

She nodded.

'Well, don't pay more than twenty-five bob a pair,' he warned. 'MacLellon's checking every penny on this production.'

Joan Waring's blue eyes twinkled.

'Has there ever been a production that he hasn't?' she retorted. 'Don't worry; I think I can get what you want for less than that.'

'That's right, my dear, get 'em as cheap as you can.' He patted her shoulder and turned away to speak to the stage manager. 'Come along to my room and we'll go through those accounts.'

He waddled across the stage in the wake of the laughing, chattering chorus girls, followed by the stage manager, and disappeared through the door at the back that led to the dressing rooms.

'Come along, Joan.' A fair-haired man came up to the girl as she was putting on her hat. 'You can help me buy my lunch.'

'Isn't your landlady catering for you?' asked the girl, powdering her nose.

He shook his head.

'No. I've got the rottenest digs in the town,' he said ruefully. 'I'm shifting on Saturday.'

'You ought to come to my place, Roger,' broke in a deep, rather pleasant voice. 'Mrs. Legge's a dear soul, and I think she'll have a room vacant on Saturday.'

'Will she?' Roger Derwent looked round at the tall, dark man who had come up behind him. 'I wish you'd fix it for me, old man.'

'I'll mention it today,' said Lionel Craig, 'and you can look in after rehearsal and fix it definitely.'

The girl had finished powdering her

nose and the three of them drifted towards the exit. Outside the stage door they paused.

'Which way are you two going?' asked Joan. 'I think I'll call in and get my shoes before lunch, then it will be done with.'

'I've got one or two things I want to get at Woolworth's so I'll come with you as far as that,' said Craig.

'Let's all go together?' suggested Roger, and they set off along the snow-powdered street towards the centre of the town. There was a short cut from the theatre to the market place and this they took. It was a narrow street, lined on either side with rather dingy-looking shops, and before one of these Craig suddenly stopped.

'I say, look at that!' he exclaimed.

'Lionel's at it again,' grinned Roger. 'What have you found this time, old man?'

Craig made no reply. He was peering intently through the dingy window of the antique shop before which he had stopped. Both Roger and the girl knew his passion for collecting what they termed junk. He carried a large trunk packed with bits and pieces he had picked up while on tour, and some of its contents were worth a lot of money.

'What have you found?' asked Roger again, and Craig pointed to the object that had taken his fancy.

It was an unframed picture, and it rested against an oak chest to the right of the window. At first glance it looked as if the artist, in a drunken fit of irresponsibility, had merely smeared his canvas with daubs of red and green paint, but as the beholder looked more closely, there emerged out of this chaos of colour the head and shoulders of a woman. She was looking straight out of the picture, her crimson lips twisted into a smile that made Joan Waring give a little inward shiver. It was the smile of a lost soul — a devilish leer that was a combination of cruelty, lust and the evil of all the ages.

'Good God, what a horrible thing!' exclaimed Roger.

'It's wonderful!' breathed Craig enthusiastically. 'Wonderful! Whoever the artist is, he's a genius. He's only used two colours, vermilion and green, and to get that effect out of so little is almost a miracle.'

'It may be very wonderful from a technical point of view, but I think it's beastly!' declared the girl.

'Beastly or not, if I can afford it I'm going to buy it,' retorted Craig. He pushed open the door of the shop and entered. A bell jangled over his head, and a little old man, with a dirty wisp of moustache, appeared behind a narrow counter, on which was displayed an assortment of objects that ranged from saucepans to statuettes. He peered at Craig through a pair of spectacles, the powerful lenses of which magnified his eyes to such an extent that he looked like an owl.

'You've got a picture in the window,' said Craig. 'How much do you want for it?'

The old man stuck his head on one side and frowned.

'Which d'yer mean?' he inquired. 'That there one with them lambs — '

'No, no!' broke in Craig hastily. 'The unframed picture — the woman's head.'

'Oh, that!' grunted the owner of the shop contemptuously. 'Ten shillin'.'

'I'll have it,' said Craig promptly — so promptly that the old man cursed inwardly for not having asked more. However, it was too late to alter his price now, so he hobbled out from behind his counter, and, reaching into the window carefully to avoid knocking over the litter of objects that stood in his way, lifted out the painting of the leering lady.

Craig paid his money and came out of the shop with his purchase, loosely wrapped in brown paper, under his arm.

'And I should keep it wrapped up if I were you,' remarked Roger. 'If your landlady sees it she'll have fits for the rest of her life.'

They reached the market place, and outside Woolworth's Craig left them with a smile and a joke — left them, although they did not know it then, for ever.

# 2

## Mr. Budd Becomes Involved

Another fall of snow began shortly before two o'clock. At half-past three it was a blizzard of scurrying white flakes, driven before a biting north-east wind. Sergeant Leek, waiting on the platform at Midchester Junction for his superior, clapped his thin hands and stamped his large feet to try and restore something like warmth to those frozen extremities. His long melancholy face was blue and pinched, and he looked even more miserable than was his wont. Presently he saw Mr. Budd, bigger and fatter than ever in the huge, fleecy overcoat he was wearing, coming towards him.

'Cold?' grunted the superintendent as he approached his shivering companion.

'Me fingers an' me feet don't seem to belong ter me,' answered the sergeant sniffing violently. 'My Lord! Ain't it cold.'

'Good seasonable weather for the time of year,' said Mr. Budd.

'Yes,' grumbled Leek. 'It's all very well on these 'ere Christmas cards, but it ain't so good when yer standin' on a draughty platform. I'm sure I've caught a chill. I can feel the wind cutting right through me!'

'The train'll be in, in a few minutes,' said Mr. Budd, 'an' then you'll be warm enough.'

'I don't think I shall ever be warm again,' complained the sergeant mournfully. 'I feel like an icicle!'

'You look like one, too!' remarked Mr. Budd unkindly. 'Don't keep on sniffing like that! Blow yer nose!'

Leek was meekly searching for a handkerchief when a loud bellow of surprise made them both turn. A large, red-faced young man, enveloped in a heavy coat, was bearing down upon them, his mouth stretched in an expansive grin of delight.

'Budd!' he cried, seizing the stout man's hand and shaking it violently. 'Budd, by all that's extraordinary! What the devil are you doing here?'

'Waitin' for the 3.45 to take me back to London, Mr. Driscoll,' answered Mr. Budd.

Driscoll shook his head.

'You may be waiting for the train, but you're not going back to London!' he declared. 'You're coming back with me to Monk's Park, that's what you're doing!'

'I'm afraid I can't do that, Mr. Driscoll,' said the big man shaking his head. 'I've got to — '

'Nonsense, you haven't got to do anything!' boomed Driscoll, his deep, bull-like roar echoing all over the platform. 'I'm not going to listen to any excuses. You've got to come and spend Christmas. D'you think I've forgotten how you saved me from losing nearly ten thousand pounds that time I was up in London?'

'I only did me duty — ' began Mr. Budd. 'The feller was a well-known confidence man — '

'He wasn't well-known to me!' interrupted Driscoll. 'Now don't argue! I've got to meet some friends of the gov'nor's, and we'll all drive back together.'

'It's very kind of you, sir,' said Mr. Budd, more than half inclined to agree, 'but what about my sergeant? He's — '

'He'll come, too, of course — plenty of room at the Park. It's a great barn of a place,' answered Driscoll. 'Well, that's settled. Here's the train!'

He jerked his head as the engine of the 3.45 swung into view round the bend through the curtain of falling snow. It came in with a hissing of steam and a squeaking grind of brakes. Porters appeared from apparently nowhere and began to shout completely unintelligible information. The engine let off steam in a prolonged and nerve-racking scream. The carriage doors opened and ten or a dozen people got out, but the friends whom Driscoll had come to meet were not among them. He darted up and down the platform, peering through the misty windows, and then came back, panting and disgusted, to where Mr. Budd and the lean sergeant were standing.

'Haven't come,' he announced unnecessarily. 'Must have missed the train.'

Whatever the reason, there was no doubt that they hadn't come, for the 3.45, with a preliminary gasp, began to grunt its way out of the station. The lighted carriages passed one by one — came to an end; there was a flash of red light, and the train vanished into the falling snow.

'There's no other train they can come by until 10.30 tonight,' grunted Driscoll. 'Dashed annoying. Come on, we'll get out of this death-trap into the warm.'

Leek breathed a prayer of thanksgiving. The north-east wind blowing along that platform was turning his bones to ice. He picked up his bag and followed Mr. Budd and Driscoll towards the exit. A big saloon car was drawn up in the station approach, and into this they got, stowing their luggage in the front seat next to the driver's. Driscoll took his place at the wheel, the engine broke into a rhythmic hum, and the car moved forward. They sped up the High Street, swung to the left, past the poster-covered front of the Theatre Royal, and into a maze of side streets that looked all alike. Half way down one of these Mr. Budd leaned forward suddenly and peered through the window.

'What's up there?' he said. 'Looks as though there was somethin' wrong.'

Driscoll slowed the car as he came abreast of the crowd that had attracted the fat superintendent's attention. A knot of people were grouped round the doorway of a house on the right, talking excitedly and gesticulating. Leek caught sight of a familiar blue uniform.

'Maybe it's an accident, or somethin' — ' he began.

'Well, it's pretty evident it's somethin',' growled Mr. Budd, and at that moment a thick-set man in a bowler hat appeared on the threshold of the house and said something to the policeman.

'Haslett, eh?' went on the superintendent. 'It's somethin' more important than an accident, or he wouldn't be there. Do you mind stoppin' a minute, Mr. Driscoll? I'd like to find out what's goin' on.'

'Carry on!' said Driscoll cheerfully. 'I'd like to know myself.'

Mr. Budd opened the door and got heavily out. The constable was endeavouring to disperse the crowd, and looked with disfavour at the big man as he approached; but his face cleared when Mr. Budd addressed the inspector, as he was on the point of re-entering the house.

'What's the matter, Haslett? What's bin happenin' here?'

Haslett turned sharply, and his pleasant face expressed surprise.

'Hello!' he exclaimed. 'I thought you'd gone back to London. What — '

'I was goin' but I didn't,' replied Mr. Budd. 'What's happened 'ere?'

The inspector's face clouded.

'Murder!' he answered briefly. 'A man named Lionel Craig — one of the people at the theatre.'

The stout superintendent looked interested.

'Murder, eh?' he murmured. 'Know who did it — '

'No,' grunted Haslett. 'It's a queer affair. I wish you'd come inside an' tell me what you think. I'd like your opinion.'

Mr. Budd nodded sleepily, and Haslett

20

led the way into the narrow, dark hall. At the foot of the stairs a thin little wisp of a woman was standing, staring at them with frightened, tear-blurred eyes.

'I'll see you in a minute, Mrs. Legget,' said the inspector kindly. 'Come up, Mr. Budd.' Followed by the fat detective, Leek, and the interested Driscoll, he mounted the stairs and approached an open door on the first landing. 'This is the room,' he said.

Mr. Budd went to the door and peered in. It was not a large room, and there was very little furniture. A bed with brass rails stood over by the wall, and this, together with an easy chair and a wardrobe, constituted the bulk. On a strip of faded carpet in the centre of the room stood a round mahogany table, on which was spread the remains of a meal, and in a chair beside this slumped the figure of a man. His head had fallen forward on the table, and his arms hung limply down at his sides, the hands loosely open. He might have been sleeping but for the dark stain that had soaked into the shabby carpet under the chair on which he sat.

'How was he killed?' asked Mr. Budd without moving from the open doorway.

'Stabbed,' answered Haslett. 'Between the shoulders. You can't see the knife from here.'

'Bin moved at all?' inquired the big man stifling a yawn.

'No.' The inspector shook his head. 'I'm waiting for the doctor to see him.'

'An' you don't know the murderer?' said Mr. Budd rubbing his chins.

'I don't know his name, but I've got a description of him,' answered the inspector. 'Not that it's going to help much,' he added irritably.

'Why?' inquired Mr. Budd.

'Because it might apply to half the population of Midchester,' replied Haslett. 'According to Mrs. Legget, Craig came home to his lunch — which, as he was a little late, she was keeping hot for him. She had just taken it up and gone back to the kitchen, when the front door bell rang. She went to the door, and found a shabbily-dressed man, whom she describes as of medium height, with a rather pale face, standing on the step. He asked to see Mr. Craig but refused to give any name, saying that Craig wouldn't know who he was, but that he wanted to see him on important business. Mrs. Leggett went up and told Craig, who was in the middle of his lunch, and Craig asked her to show the man up. She did so, and then hurried back to the kitchen, where a smell of burning warned her that her own lunch was spoiling. Twenty minutes later she heard the front door open and shut, and concluded that her lodger's visitor had gone. She thought no more of the matter, had her lunch, and made herself a cup of tea. At half-past three she went up to Craig's room to make up the fire, believing that he had gone back to the theatre. She found him — like that!' He nodded towards the figure in the chair. 'She ran out screaming for the police, and that's all she can tell us.'

Mr. Budd frowned.

'And that ain't a lot,' he remarked. 'It doesn't look as though this feller, Craig was expectin' any trouble from his visitor.'

'You mean that if he had been, he

wouldn't have invited him up?' said Haslett.

'No, I don't mean that exactly,' answered Mr. Budd. 'But when this man was shown up, Craig was in the middle of 'is lunch. If you look at the table you'll see that he had finished it before he was killed. Which means that he must 'ave gone on eatin' it while his visitor was with 'im. If he'd bin afraid of 'im he wouldn't have done that.'

'Yes, I see,' agreed Haslett. 'That's a good point.'

'Either Craig knew the man,' went on Mr. Budd, 'or he regarded him as a stranger who was perfectly harmless.'

'If he was a stranger,' said Driscoll, 'why did he commit the murder?'

'It's no use tryin' to guess that until somethin' more is known of Craig,' answered Mr. Budd. 'The motive will prob'ly give us the killer. You're sure there's nothin' more to be got from Mrs. Legget?' He turned to Haslett.

'You can see her if you like,' said the inspector, 'but I don't think so.' He went to the door and called.

The thin little woman came hurriedly, her bird-like face with its frightened eyes turning from one to the other.

'I'd just like to ask you a few questions,' began Mr. Budd gently.

'I don't know nuthin' more'n than what I've already told the h'inspector,' she broke in quickly. 'I never see the feller before in me life.'

'Nobody's suggestin' you did, m'am,' said Mr. Budd soothingly. 'The questions I want to ask you concern Mr. Craig. Now, what sort of a feller was he?'

'As nice a man as ever drew the breath o' life,' declared the landlady rapidly. 'Why anyone should 'ave wanted to kill 'im I don't know — though I did warn 'im!'

'You warned him?' said the big man sharply. 'What did you warn 'im about?'

'Bringin' that 'orrible pitcher into the 'ouse,' said Mrs. Legget tearfully. 'I told 'im no good 'ud come of it, and it ain't.'

'What picture are you talkin' about?' asked Mr. Budd.

' 'E bought it this morning,' answered the landlady. ' 'E was always buyin' things

25

— sort of an 'obby it was. I said it 'ud bring 'im bad luck as soon as 'e showed it to me.'

'What was it?' persisted the superintendent.

'An 'orrible thing!' answered Mrs. Leggett. 'When you first looked at it, you couldn't see nuthin' 'cept a mess o' red an' green paint, an' then a woman's 'ead seemed to grow out at yer if yer know what I mean. A dreadful leerin' smile she 'ad, too — called 'er the leerin' lady. You can see it fer yourself. 'E put it on the mantelpiece in there.'

She pointed to the open door of the bed sitting room.

Mr. Budd, with his eyes very wide open, crossed the landing and peered in.

'There ain't no picture here now, he said.

'Well then 'e must 'ave put it away,' asserted the landlady. 'It was there when I took in 'is lunch, 'cause it was then 'e showed it to me.'

'Was it there when you showed this other feller in?' asked Mr. Budd, and she nodded.

'Yes, it was — I'm positive,' she said.

With the help of Leek and Haslett the big man made a quick but thorough search of the room.

'Well,' he said, when they had finished, 'there ain't any picture here now.'

There could only be one explanation. The murderer had taken the picture away with him!

# 3

## What Silas Mann Knew

Mr. Oswald Hope glanced irritably at his watch, his round face crinkled with annoyance.

'What the devil can have happened to the man?' he growled. 'It's all very well to be a few minutes late, but when it comes to hours — ' He snorted expressively.

'We left Mr. Craig in the market place,' volunteered Joan Waring. 'He was going straight home then — after he'd done his shopping. Perhaps he's been taken ill, or — '

'God knows what's happened to him!' snapped the little producer with more truth than he knew. 'All I know is that he's holding up this rehearsal.' He swung round to the stage manager. 'Send someone along to his digs, will you.'

He stopped as the aged stage door-keeper appeared through the door at the back of the stage. He looked about him questioningly; and then, catching sight of the producer in the stalls, came down to the footlights and called across to him.

'There's four gents ter see yer,' he announced.

'Four gents — I don't know any gents!' growled the harassed Mr. Hope. 'Who are they? What do they want? Whatever it is I can't see 'em!'

He dismissed the 'four gents' with a wave of his chubby hand. But the stage doorkeeper was persistent.

'They say it's very h'important,' he mumbled. 'One of em's Inspector 'Aslett.'

'The Police?' Roger Derwent spoke, and his face changed. 'By Jove, do you think it can be anything to do with Craig? Perhaps he's met with an accident. Been run over or something.'

Mr. Hope's irritability vanished and he looked grave.

'There's something in that,' he muttered. 'All right, Tubbs, I'll come.'

He joined the bent-backed Tubbs, and they went out through the exit together. A silence settled down on the little groups of people on the stage. Something, perhaps it was a premonition, struck the usual chatter from their lips, and left them a waiting and expectant crowd. Even the chorus had, for once, ceased giggling and whispering under their breath. And they had not long to wait. Barely ten minutes passed before a white-faced, worried Oswald Hope re-appeared in the stalls accompanied by the four callers; a very fat man with sleepy-looking eyes; a broad-shouldered, red-faced young man; a lean, miserable-looking man; and a man who had police officer written all over him.

'I'm afraid, ladies and gentlemen, something dreadful has happened.' Mr. Hope's voice was even more than usually husky, and had acquired a slight stammer. 'Craig has been — murdered!'

He jerked the last word out as though it was a plum stone that had stuck in his throat and he had difficulty in extricating it.

'Murder!'

The ominous word ran from lip to lip; was caught up and wafted to the flies, and came echoing back from the black depths of the empty theatre.

'Murder!' Joan Waring's ashen lips murmured the word, and then turned big, wide, horror-filled eyes to Roger Derwent, who was staring with a fixed and incredulous stare at Mr. Oswald Hope.

'What Mr. Hope has just told you is true,' said Inspector Haslett gravely. 'Mr. Lionel Craig was discovered this afternoon, stabbed to death in his lodgings in Little Salt Street.'

'But — but — ' Roger passed his tongue over his dry lips. 'It seems impossible. Only a few hours ago he was laughing and joking . . . '

'It's true, all the same, sir,' said the inspector. 'We have come here to make a few inquiries about him. This is Superintendent Budd, of the C.I.D. He was in Midchester investigating another matter, and has very kindly offered to assist me in this case.'

A rustle like the wind passing over dead leaves ran round the people present. It was the relaxing of the tension caused by the news of Lionel Craig's violent death.

The rustle grew in volume, and then everybody started speaking at once — jerkily, disjointedly. Mr. Budd held up a fat protesting hand.

'One of you at a time, please,' he said, and the silence fell again. 'Now I understand that Mr. Craig left this theatre this afternoon at a quarter to one. Is that right?'

'That's right,' Oswald Hope confirmed the statement with a nod.

'He did not arrive at his lodging until a quarter to two,' went on Mr. Budd. 'Can anyone tell me what he did in the interval?'

'He left the theatre with us,' said Joan. 'Mr. Derwent and I were going shopping, and Mr. Craig came with us.'

'I see,' murmured the big man. 'Were you with him when he bought a picture?'

The girl nodded.

'Yes,' she said. 'Mr. Craig bought it at a little shop near here. He was always buying things like that.'

'Could you take us to the shop, miss?' asked Mr. Budd.

'Yes, of course I could,' she answered.

'Why are you so anxious to find the shop?' broke in Derwent. 'What has it got to do with Craig's death?'

'Maybe nothin' — maybe a lot,' said the superintendent. 'The picture's got somethin' ter do with it anyway.'

'The picture?' The girl looked at him in bewilderment.

'The picture,' repeated Mr. Budd. 'It was stolen by the murderer. At the moment it seems to 'ave bin the only motive for the crime.'

'Good God!' exclaimed Roger. 'How on earth — '

'It's no good askin' me that, sir, because I don't know,' said Mr. Budd wearily. 'Would you mind, Mr. Hope, if Miss — ' He paused doubtfully.

'Miss Waring,' said the producer.

'Would you mind if Miss Waring showed us this shop?'

'Not at all, not at all,' replied Mr. Hope quickly. 'Go along, my dear.'

They waited while the girl put on her hat and coat, and then, leaving Inspector Haslett to question the rest of the company, left the theatre with her.

A few minutes' walk brought them to the little shop where Lionel Craig had made his ill-fated purchase. A dim light gleamed through the dirty window, and they could see the figure of the old proprietor moving about behind the littered counter. Mr. Budd pushed open the door and entered. When the bell had ceased jangling, he addressed the old man, who had leaned forward at his entrance.

'I want you to give me some information,' he said. 'A friend of mine bought a picture here this afternoon.'

'Um,' grunted the old man. 'Well, what about it?'

'How did it come into your possession?' said Mr. Budd.

'I bought it,' was the reply. 'How d'yer think anything comes inter my possession?'

The stout superintendent ignored the surliness of his tone.

'When did you buy it?' he asked.

'Day afore yesterday!' snapped the other. 'Look 'ere, mister, wot are you gettin' at?' His small eyes narrowed and

34

he looked suspiciously at his questioner.

'I'm a bit interested in that picture,' answered Mr. Budd. 'Who painted it?'

'Don't know. It hadn't got no name to it.' The shopkeeper was getting a little fed up, and showed it.

'D'yer know the person who sold it to you?' persisted Mr. Budd.

'No, I don't!' snarled the old man. 'An' if you ain't got nuthin' better ter do than waste yer time, I 'ave!'

He turned away with, the obvious intention of concluding the interview, but Mr. Budd had other ideas.

'Listen here!' he said sharply. 'If you don't answer my questions here, maybe you'll have to answer 'em in a less pleasant place.'

'Wotcher mean?' said the old man uneasily.

'I'm a police officer,' said Mr. Budd, and the effect of this was electrical. The wizened face changed, and a look of alarm crept into the beady, red-rimmed eyes. The owner of the little antique shop was frightened. He was only too willing to tell all he knew, which wasn't much.

The picture had been brought to his shop by a small, shrivelled-up man, who stated that he was starving. At first Silas Mann — for that was his name, it appeared — had refused to buy it. It was not the kind of thing that was likely to have a ready sale in the district, and his shop was fairly full up as it was. But the man had pleaded so hard that at last Mr. Mann had offered him half-a-crown for the thing. He had eagerly accepted, grabbed the money, and gone. Mr. Mann had never seen him before or since.

Such was the whole of his information, and it wasn't very helpful. Mr. Budd left the shop after a few more questions, feeling rather disappointed. The next step was to trace the man who had sold the picture to Mr. Mann, and it didn't look as if it would be too easy.

At least that was Mr. Budd's conclusion at the time, but it turned out otherwise.

# 4

## The Light in the Dark House

Midchester had plenty to talk about that evening, for the news of the murder of Lionel Craig ran through the town like wildfire. The landlord of the Crown and Anchor confided his theories about 'these 'ere theatre people' to a select gathering of cronies, and dispensed much liquid refreshment. The editor of the *Midchester Times* prepared a special front page 'splash' for the morning edition, and in every house, cottage, and mansion interest in the advent of Christmas was for the moment forgotten and Murder took prior place.

The snow had ceased falling shortly after seven o'clock, and the night was cold and frosty — one of those hard, glassy nights when one's breath is like steam and every footfall rings and echoes.

Mr. Budd, washing himself leisurely in the big, warm bedroom which had been

37

allotted to him at Monk's Park, finished drying his face and hands and looked out the window across the snow-covered lawn towards the white expanse of countryside that lay beyond. His forehead was wrinkled in a thoughtful frown, and, if the truth must be told, he saw nothing of the scene that spread itself before him, although it was well worth looking at. His mind was completely occupied with the strange crime which accident had thrown in his path. But for the meeting with Driscoll and his acceptance of that boisterous individual's invitation, he and Leek would have been on their way to London when the murder was discovered. He sighed and carefully brushed his thinning hair. Those sort of things happened, and it was an interesting business anyway.

Neither he nor Inspector Haslett had succeeded in learning anything further at the theatre. Craig had apparently been a hard-working, steady sort of fellow, with only one vice — if it could be called a vice — that of collecting old and out-of-the-way objects. The trunk at his lodgings in

Little Salt Street had been packed full of all sorts of curios, but nothing had come to light that was applicable to his death, or that offered the slightest suggestion as to the identity of his murderer. He had, according to Mr. Oswald Hope, a small flat in London, and Mr. Budd had wired to the Yard to make detailed inquiries into Craig's past, and to find out everything that was known about him. Not that he expected any very sensational discovery from this. He was convinced that the solution to the mystery of his death lay not in Craig, but in the picture, which the murderer had taken away with him. Craig was nothing more than a pawn in the game. He had got in the way when he had bought that picture, and having got in the way, he had been swept out of it. Mr. Budd felt pretty sure that if he had not bought that picture, he would never have been killed. For some reason unknown the murderer had wanted that picture so badly that he had not hesitated to kill to gain possession of it. It was a queer business. Whoever the murderer was, he must have witnessed the purchase of the painting by Craig, otherwise he wouldn't have known that it was in his possession. And if he had, why hadn't he gone in and bought the thing himself? A very queer business certainly.

The opening of the door and the arrival of Leek put an end to his reverie. The lean sergeant was shining with soap, and for once seemed to be almost cheerful.

'Nice place this, ain't it?' he remarked. 'I'm glad we came.'

'Then my happiness is complete!' grunted Mr. Budd. 'I was gettin' worried as to whether you might be enjoyin' yerself or not.'

'You couldn't 'elp but enjoy yerself in a place like this,' answered Leek seriously. 'It must 'ave cost a bit.'

Mr. Budd made an unintelligible reply, and the dinner gong sounding at that moment they went down.

Old John Driscoll was pleased to meet them, and said so. He thanked Mr. Budd profusely for saving his son from the wiles of the confidence man during his visit to London — so profusely, indeed that the stout superintendent was embarrassed.

40

They were a bachelor party, for the old mill owner was a widower, and the friends who had been expected, and had included a nephew of the old man's and two nieces, had wired to say that, owing to illness, they would be unable to come after all.

'You know,' remarked the silver-haired old man, when the coffee had been served in the big library, 'this murder interests me tremendously.'

'It interests me, too, sir,' answered Mr. Budd from the depths of an enormous armchair. 'It's a very queer business.'

'The point that puzzles me,' went on his host, 'is the picture. It seems such a ridiculous reason for killing a man.'

'It does, don't it?' agreed the stout detective. 'So far as I can make out the thing had no value — no money value, I mean. It might 'ave bin of value from an artistic angle . . . '

'You don't think,' broke in the booming voice of young Driscoll, 'that Craig may have been murdered by a madman?'

Mr. Budd pursed his lips.

'Well, it isn't impossible, of course,' he

41

murmured. 'But I'd want to exhaust all other explanations before I came to that one.'

'What were you thinking about when you made that suggestion, Jack?' said the white-haired man, eyeing his son keenly. 'Amos Grant?'

Young Driscoll reddened, and laughed.

'Well — yes — as a matter of fact I was,' he admitted. 'I suppose it was the association of ideas that made me think of him. The picture — and . . . '

'Who is Amos Grant?' inquired Mr. Budd.

'Say, rather, who *was* Amos Grant,' answered his host.

'Well, then, who was Amos Grant?' said the stout man.

'Two years ago he was the sole topic of conversation in Midchester,' replied Driscoll, 'as, I've no doubt, the murder is at the present moment. He was the owner of the Lodge which, since his death has been called the Dark House.'

'That sounds like an interestin' story, sir,' said Mr. Budd.

'It is,' the elder Driscoll nodded. 'A

very interesting story. The Grants of Midchester were a very old family, and the Lodge has been in their possession for generations — until now. It's in nobody's possession now except the rats and the mice.' He stopped and flicked the ash from his cigar. 'I'll tell you the story if you're interested,' he went on. 'Amos Grant inherited the estate from his father, Jonathan Grant, about twenty-five years ago. It was worth, altogether, round about three hundred and fifty thousand pounds. Amos was then twenty-eight, and for most of his life had lived in Paris. After the death of his father he came to Midchester and took up his residence at the Lodge. He was very popular from the first, and was entertained a lot and generally feted. He was the last of his line, and everybody wondered when, and whom, he would marry.

'Well, they didn't have to wonder long, for it very soon became evident Beryl Fairfax was the lady of his choice. She was the daughter of Geoffery Fairfax, and the Fairfaxes were as old a family as the Grants — if anything, a little older.

Everyone thought that it would be an excellent match — Beryl and Amos were always in each other's company, went everywhere together, and, to cut a long story short, were married eighteen months later. The marriage was apparently a success. Amos was devoted to his young wife, and so far as outward appearances went, she was devoted to him. They were alluded to as an ideal couple. Then suddenly, and without warning the crash came. Beryl left her husband and ran away with the manager of the Theatre Royal, a man called Carstairs.

'Amos Grant was distracted. For months he was so ill that his life was despaired of by the doctors, and when he eventually recovered he shut himself up in the Lodge, dismissed all the servants with the exception of one old man, and never set foot outside the place again. The house was left to fall into decay; the grounds, which had been so trim and well-kept, became weed-choked. Its whole appearance was a reflection on the change that had come over its owner. At first a few of his more intimate friends tried to

interfere, but they received no encourage-
ment. Amos refused to see anyone, callers
were turned away by the old man who
acted as his servant, or got no answer at
all to their ringing and knocking, and
presently the people, who had tried their
best, gave it up as a bad job, and Amos
was left to himself.

'Every day the old servant — Snellkins
was his name — would go into the town
and do whatever shopping that was
necessary. He always had a list written
out, and never spoke to a soul. This went
on until two years ago, when suddenly he
was missed. At first the shopkeepers
thought he was ill when he failed to put
in his usual appearance, but after a week
had elapsed they mentioned the matter
to the police. Your friend Haslett paid a
visit to the Lodge, but could get no
answer to his knocking and ringing.
Eventually the place was broken into and
they found Amos dead in his bed.

'There was no sign of the servant,
Snellkins, except that the state of his
room suggested that he had hastily
packed. Amos had been dead for several

days, and the doctor stated that he had died from heart failure. An investigation into his affairs showed that there was no will, nor was there anything left, seemingly, of his fortune of three hundred and fifty thousand pounds. This had been invested in various ways, but inquiries revealed that he had for years been converting it into cash, but what he had done with it nobody knew.

'It wasn't at his bank. His balance there was less than five pounds, and he hadn't drawn a cheque for years. Neither was there any money in the house, though a thorough search was made. The police theory was that old Snellkins had gone off with it; but the old man was never traced, and the money was never found. That's roughly the story. The house has been shut up and empty ever since — a dark, miserable pile, dirty and neglected, and haunted, so people say, by the ghost of Amos Grant. You can see the place from your bedroom window.'

'Um,' commented Mr. Budd, when he finished. 'A queer story, an' interestin' — very interestin'. Was anythin' ever heard of the wife?'

Driscoll shook his head.

'No. She was advertised for at Amos's death,' he replied, 'but she never came forward. Her brother, Charles Fairfax, who still lives at the Chase, is under the impression that she's dead. He's no proof, of course, but I should think it was quite likely.'

Mr. Budd pinched his thick lower lip and looked across at young Driscoll.

'When you made the suggestion that Craig was killed by a madman, what made you think of this feller, Amos Grant?' he asked. But Driscoll could only repeat that it was an association of ideas. Grant had been an artist during his youth and the theatre was mixed up with both the murder and Grant's story, and Grant had definitely been crazy.

'Um, I see,' said Mr. Budd when this explanation had been given him and the subject was dropped.

Both he and Leek went to bed early. The stout superintendent, however, did not immediately undress. Pulling up a chair to the cosy fire, he lit one of his strong black cigars and thought over the events of the day.

He was in the act of removing his jacket, preparatory to going to bed when his thoughts returned to the story of Amos Grant and the Dark House. Old Driscoll had said that he could see the place from his window. Pulling aside the heavy curtains, he looked out across the frozen landscape, gleaming in the light of the pale moon. Away in the distance the dark mass of the old house loomed black and sinister against the snow. And then as he looked Mr. Budd stiffened, and his heavy-lidded eyes narrowed. Was that the reflection of moonlight on the glass of a window? No. There was a light in the Dark House!

# 5

## 'Red Light'

Across the white carpet of snow Mr. Budd stared at that flickering pinpoint of light.

There was no mistaking, now, what it was. Somebody was in that desolate house with a candle. Who were they, and what were they doing? The big man glanced at his watch. Ten minutes past twelve. His brows drew together in a frown. Here was something odd; very odd indeed!

Of course, there was the possibility that the light merely indicated that some unfortunate tramp had taken refuge from the bitter cold for the night. It was the most likely and the most sensible explanation; but . . .

That devouring curiosity that was such a large part of Mr. Budd's character was getting the upper hand, and in less than a minute from the time when he had first seen the light he had made up his mind. He would go and see for himself who this midnight occupant of the otherwise empty house was. If it was only a tramp — well, no harm would be done; and if it was not, then he was very anxious to see who it was and what they were doing.

The story told him by old Driscoll came surging up into his brain. What had happened to the servant, Snellkins? Had he gone off with that three hundred and fifty thousand pounds in solid cash, or had just been scared at finding his master dead, and gone — without the money? Was it still somewhere concealed in that pile of rotting wood and brick that was called the Dark House?

For the moment Mr. Budd had forgotten the murder of Craig and the picture he had never seen, and his whole mind was fixed on discovering the meaning of this flickering light that still shone out from the uncurtained window of the Dark House.

He wrapped a thick scarf round his throat and dragged on his heavy overcoat. Quietly he opened his bedroom door and stepped out into the blackness of the corridor. The whole house was still and silent and sleeping. He paused for an instant in the darkness, debating whether he should wake Leek, and then decided that it would only be a waste of time. The sergeant would have to dress and he wasn't very quick at the best of times.

A brilliant shaft of light cut the darkness and quivered, a white, wavering pool, on the carpet of the passage as he pressed the button of his torch, and by its light he guided himself to the head of the staircase. The hall below was a black cavern that yawned before him as he went carefully down the stairs.

It took him some time to draw back the bolts and unfasten the chain at the front door, but presently he had the door open and stepped out into the cold air of the night. The snow lay thickly, soft and powdery, so that he sank ankle deep at every step. Slowly he made his way across the lawn — a black blot on the surrounding whiteness — until he came to the belt of shrubbery that divided the grounds of Monk's Park from the meadows beyond There was a wire fence behind the bushes and this he laboriously climbed. Crossing the meadowland was the most difficult part of his journey, for the snow, here, had piled up in unexpected drifts; but he managed it, and at last found himself within the rank, unkempt grounds of the Dark House. The trees grew very thickly, and their branches had acted as a partial screen to the falling snow, so that it was easier going. He came to the front door with his feet and halfway up his legs soaking wet, but otherwise unharmed. And the front door was open!

He gave a swift glance down the white ribbon of the drive, and frowned. Marking its smooth surface were footprints, not one line as he had expected, but two! So there were two people in the old house. Mr. Budd went over to the footprints and peered at them. Two people had come to the house, but they had not come together. One — the owner apparently of a rather large foot — had come several minutes after the other. It was easy to read that on that snowy page.

The first comer's footprints — a smaller foot — had started to thaw. Big-foot had left prints with sharply defined edges, which obliterated them in places. Interesting and peculiar, thought Mr. Budd, and queer. Small-foot had come to the Dark House, gone in, and then Big-foot had followed him later.

The big man went back to the door and listened. He could hear from somewhere within the faint sound of voices whispering. He crossed the threshold and stood within the blackness of the hall. The smell of decay reached his nostrils — that musty smell which is part of the atmosphere of a long-deserted house. The voices came from somewhere above, and Mr. Budd made his way cautiously towards the staircase. He had his foot on the first stair when there was a sudden scuffling noise, and a scream — a scream that started shrilly and ended in a little gurgling grunt.

Careless of the noise he made, now, Mr. Budd pounded up the stairs as fast as he could.

A light streamed out from a partly open door on the first landing, and as he reached

53

the topmost stair, a huge shadow, grotesquely thrown by the light within, loomed across the door. The crouching figure of a man appeared on the threshold, a shapeless, distorted figure that was unrecognisable in that dim light.

Mr. Budd heard a guttural oath break from startled lips, and then the emerging figure was on him. He went down under the impact with a thud that knocked all the breath out of him, and his attacker pulled himself free and stumbled hurriedly down the stairs.

Mr. Budd struggled to his feet, bruised, dazed, and gasping — and leaned against the wall. He was a heavy man and the fall had shaken him. Gradually he regained both his breath and his steadiness. It was useless going after the man who had attacked him, he would be well away by now. A sound from the room with the open door turned his attention to the man who still remained in the house — a bubbling gasp, almost a groan. Mr. Budd moved unsteadily over to the door and looked in. The room was small and bare. On the dusty boards a candle burned unevenly in a pool of its own grease. It cast a dancing light dimly over the room, and revealed a man lying in a doubled up position under the window. He was moving painfully, and from under him came a sluggish stream of red that mingled with the dust on the floor . . .

Mr. Budd went forward and knelt down beside him. The blood was welling from a gash in the side of his neck, and it only required a glance to see that he was dying. He turned a pair of fast-glazing eyes up at the big man and his lips moved. No sound came, however, and he fell back. Mr. Budd thought he was dead, but he made another supreme effort to speak and this time managed to gasp out two words. 'Red . . . light . . . ' He jerked his head weakly towards the door and then a sound like the escape of water from a washbasin left his throat. His head fell sideways and he was suddenly still, with that uncanny stillness which is death.

Mr. Budd looked round in the direction in which he had nodded.

Leaning up against the wall behind the door was the picture of the Leering Lady!

# 6

## The Identity of the Portrait

'I must admit,' said Inspector Haslett, 'that I'm all at sea. This latest development has made things worse than they were before,'

'Maybe it has, and then again maybe it hasn't,' grunted Mr. Budd. 'At least we know somethin' more'n what we did yesterday.'

The inspector shrugged his shoulders.

'But what does it mean?' he demanded.

'That I can't tell you,' said Mr. Budd slowly.

It was ten o'clock on the morning following the big man's discovery at the Dark House, and he, Leek, and Haslett were seated in the breakfast room at Monk's Park, drinking hot coffee.

After having assured himself that the man was dead, Mr. Budd had taken the picture of the Leering Lady and gone

56

back to Monk's Park, from whence he had telephoned to the local police station. Haslett had, of course, gone home, but when the stout superintendent had impressed upon the Sergeant-in-charge the urgency of finding him, a constable had been dispatched to his home.

A thorough investigation of the Dark House and the body had resulted in no clue to the identity of the murderer. There was, however, little doubt that the dead man was the person who had sold the picture to Silas Mann, for as soon as it was possible to do so they had brought that aged and grumbling individual from his shop to the Dark House, and he had identified him without hesitation. But who he was there was no means of telling. His ragged clothes contained nothing that provided even a suggestion as to his name, or where he came from.

That he was not the man who had killed Craig seemed certain, for Mrs. Legget, also brought along by the police, was vehement about this. The dead man was as much a mystery as was his presence in the Dark House — as much a mystery as the man who had stabbed him.

Which of them had taken the picture there, it was impossible to say, but it seemed most likely to have been taken there by the murderer. Unless the dead man was an accomplice of the killer he wouldn't have had the picture. It all came back to the picture. Mr. Budd was sure that that was at the bottom of the whole queer business.

Some further light might be shed if they could discover the identity of the dead man, and, with this object in view, his fingerprints had been taken and sent to Scotland Yard, and a full description circulated for newspaper publication.

The doctor who had examined the body had been able to state one thing definitely. The man had been half starved. He was little more than skin and bone, and his last meal had been eaten some forty-eight hours before his death. They had got thus far in the investigation when they had paused for a welcome break and hot coffee at Monk's Park.

'What I should like to know,' remarked

Inspector Haslett, taking a genteel sip at his coffee, 'is what those two men were doing at the Dark House at all.'

'If we knew that,' answered Mr. Budd, with a prodigious yawn, 'we'd have solved more than half the mystery. What I should like to know is how the picture comes into it.'

'Wish I could suggest something,' grunted Haslett, shaking his head; 'but I can't. What was it that fellow said just before he died? 'Red light'. What the devil did he mean by that?'

'Ask me another!' replied Mr. Budd, feeling in his pocket for one of his thin, black cigars. 'There wasn't any red light in the house. Maybe it was his way of sayin' 'Danger'.'

'Sounds more like delirium, ter me,' put in Leek. 'People say lots o' funny things when they're dyin'.'

'And when they ain't!' snapped the big man. 'I don't think it was delirium at all; I think he was tryin' ter tell me somethin' important.'

'But what?' demanded Haslett impatiently. 'What sense can you make of 'red light'?'

'Maybe when we know a bit more it'll be plain what 'e was gettin' at,' said Mr. Budd.

'A bit more!' echoed the inspector. 'A bit more! A devil of a lot more if you ask me!'

There was silence. Mr. Budd blew out a cloud of strong, evil-smelling smoke, and gazed up at the ceiling.

'Do you remember the story of Amos Grant?' he asked suddenly.

Haslett looked at him in astonishment.

'Yes,' he answered. 'But what the deuce has that got to do — '

'Maybe nothin' at all,' replied Mr. Budd dreamily. 'But I've got a theory — '

'It isn't theories we want,' interrupted the inspector. 'It's facts!'

'My theory deals with facts,' said the stout man. 'Three hundred and fifty thousand facts, which have vanished into thin air.'

Haslett started.

'You mean the money — ' he began, and Mr. Budd nodded.

'But it's generally believed that the old man, Snellkins, went off with that.'

'There was no proof that he did,' said Mr. Budd gently.

'Well, what happened to it, then?' demanded the inspector. 'If you imagine that it's hidden somewhere in that house, you're wrong! That was the first thing that occurred to me at the time, and the place was thoroughly searched.'

'I'm not suggestin' that it's hidden in the house,' said Mr. Budd. 'But I am suggestin' that it's hidden somewhere.'

'If it had been we should have found it,' grunted Haslett stubbornly. 'You can take it from me that Snellkins got away with it.'

'Well, well,' said Mr. Budd amiably, 'maybe he did. But for the sake of argument, let's suppose he didn't. Let's suppose that Grant, after he had con- verted 'is prop'ty into cash, hid it somewhere — choosin' his hidin' place so carefully that nobody could find it. Let's suppose that this Snellkins knew this, but didn't know the actual hidin' place, an' that when 'e left so hurriedly after the death of the feller, 'e left with empty hands. Let's suppose that he mentioned to someone that this great sum o' money was somewhere in existence, an' that this someone 'e mentioned it to decided to try an' find it. Let's suppose all that an' see where it gets us.'

'It doesn't get us anywhere,' said Haslett. 'Except up against a blank wall. If you're trying to connect the murder of this man Craig and this unknown fellow at the Dark House with Amos Grant and his money you're going to have all your work cut out.'

'It's connected already,' murmured Mr. Budd. 'The picture an' the man who originally sold it were both found at the Dark House.'

'Yes, but only because it *was* the Dark House,' retorted the inspector. 'These people knew that nobody ever went near the place and chose it for that reason. I admit I don't know how the picture comes into it, but I think they met to talk things over — quarrelled, and one killed the other.'

'Then why didn't they both go to the house together?' demanded the stout man. 'Why did the murdered man come first an' the other feller after him?'

Haslett's face broke into a smile.

'That's an easy one,' he said. 'They arranged to meet there, and one was a little early. That's simple.'

'Well, here's somethin' that's not so simple,' said Mr. Budd. 'What's the secret of the picture, an' why did one of 'em bring it to the Dark House last night?'

'How can I tell you that?' began Haslett in protest.

'If you agree with my theory, you can anyway offer an idea,' broke in the big man.

Sergeant Leek leaned suddenly forward, his long face alight with excitement.

'I see what yer getting' at,' he said surprisingly. 'These 'ere people was lookin' fer the money, an' the pitcher 'as somethin' ter do with it.'

'What's 'appened to you?' said Mr. Budd. 'That's the first time for years that I've known you make a really sensible remark!'

Leek's sallow face reddened with pleasure at this unexpected praise, but Haslett snorted.

'How could the picture help them?' he

said. 'We've examined it carefully and it's just an ordinary painting. There's nothing about it at all that could possibly tell them where this money is — even if it's anywhere.'

'The thing is that picture ain't just an ordinary paintin'. It's a most extraordinary paintin',' declared Mr. Budd. 'I'll bet you've never seen anythin' like it before in yer life.'

'I don't know much about paintings,' answered the inspector, 'but I think all this is too far-fetched. However, s'pose we have another look at the thing?'

Without waiting for a reply, he got up and fetched the picture of the Leering Lady, which was resting against the wall, wrapped in brown paper, and brought it over to the table. He took off the covering and they all three bent over the daub.

The face of the woman stared up at them mockingly, and the twisted lips seemed to curl back still farther in that curious leering smile.

'You see,' remarked Haslett, 'there's nothing to bear out your idea, and there's no frame in which anything could have been concealed. The back of the canvas is blank, too — if there was any clue to the hiding place of the money it would have to be in the actual painting itself, and you can see there's nothing of the sort.'

They were so absorbed that they did not hear the door open and the elder Driscoll enter, and were completely unaware of his presence until he spoke.

'You look busy,' he remarked pleasantly. 'What's that you're looking at? The famous picture, which is at the root of all the fuss? I should like to see it.'

He approached the table, and Leek made way for him.

'I know something about art — ' he began, and stopped, staring down at the face of the Leering Lady with dropped jaw and startled eyes.

'Good God!' he breathed huskily, and again: 'Good God!'

'What's the matter?' asked Mr. Budd, and Driscoll pulled himself together.

'Do you remember the story of Amos Grant I told you last night?' he said, and when the big man nodded: 'You remember I told you he married Beryl Fairfax, and that she ran away with a man called Carstairs?'

'Well?' said Mr. Budd, but he knew what was coming.

'That is Beryl Fairfax,' said Driscoll shortly.

# 7

## The Brother

The man at the window gazed out across the snowbound grounds within range of his sight; his eyes in their hollow sockets, vacant and lifeless.

The room in which he stood was lined with books — old books, tier upon tier of them, ranging from the polished floor to the raftered ceiling. Books, whose bindings were not tooled yesterday nor many yesterdays before that, and whose leaves were yellowing under the hand of time.

It was a comfortable room with shabby furniture — ancient like the books, and gleaming with the polish that only years can provide. The keynote of the whole place was age, with the exception of the man by the window. He was only fifty, but his face was lined with care. Across his forehead and between his eyes, worry had carved its tracks, almost as deeply as those tracks his eyes could see marring the virgin whiteness of the snow.

The Fairfaxes had never been rich, and Charles Fairfax — this man who stood so still and silent by the window — was definitely poor; was so poor that the spectre of actual want hovered constantly at his elbow.

The house, and all it contained, had been mortgaged to the last stone and book by his father, whose foolish speculations had eaten away what money there had been, and brought him, a broken man, to a premature death.

Charles Fairfax, the last of the line, raised a hand to his lips, and began to nibble at his nails. It was an unconscious habit when he was worried, and the fact that the nails were bitten to the quicks spoke for itself. Most of his worries were locked up in the broad, leather-topped writing table that filled the centre of the room.

A letter from the bank, still polite, but very firm; a letter from the solicitors concerning the interest due on the mortgage, very much firmer, and not at all polite. Bills from here, and bills from there; some of his own debts; others — the majority — relics of his father's prodigality — on nothing.

The lean jaw moved restlessly, and the white teeth gnawed at the fingertips. Three days to Christmas, and on the twenty-fourth the interest on the mortgage was due. If it was not paid — Charles Fairfax shivered and moved away from the window. The mortgagees would foreclose, and the house that he loved — the house in which he had been born — would be sold under the hammer.

The dark eyes in their cave-like sockets gleamed; the lean jaw hardened, and the lines round the thin lips deepened. There was character in the face — nothing of the weakling.

Up and down the long room he paced — back and forth — a ceaseless, restless promenade, as ceaseless and restless as the brain behind those burning eyes. There was the faint, discordant jangle of a bell, but he heard nothing, so occupied was he with his own unpleasant thoughts.

A tap came on the door, and an elderly woman entered — the woman who, together with her daughter, was all that remained of the once imposing staff of servants. He heard her, and swung round.

'Well?'

The word burst from his lips like the firing of a bullet.

'There are two gentlemen, sir — ' began the woman.

'Who are they?' snapped Charles Fairfax. 'I can't see anybody. I told you I couldn't see anybody.'

'One of 'em's Inspector 'Aslett,' said the housekeeper.

She held out a card. He almost snatched the pasteboard from her fingers, and glared at the inscribed name.

'All right; ask them in,' he said briefly.

The woman retired, and the strong hand, with its bitten fingers, closed over the card. The fingers ground it, a crumpled ruin, into the palm. Charles Fairfax stared at the door. Presently it opened again, and the elderly woman ushered in Haslett and Mr. Budd.

'Good morning, Mr. Fairfax,' greeted

the inspector, and waited. But Charles Fairfax remained silent. 'I'm sorry to disturb you, but I believe you can help us. This is Superintendent Budd, of New Scotland Yard.'

The burning eyes fixed themselves on the big man, and met a sleepy gaze. The head inclined — a perceptible bow. The lips remained motionless. There was an awkward pause.

'I should like to ask you one or two questions, sir.' Mr. Budd broke the silence pleasantly. 'We're inquirin' into this murder — '

'You are referring to the death of the actor man?' interrupted Fairfax.

'Yes, sir,' said Mr. Budd. 'An' also the man who was killed in the Dark House last night.'

'I know nothing about a man having been killed in the Dark House,' said Fairfax. 'What makes you think that I should know anything about either of these deaths?'

'Well, sir, I'll explain,' said Mr. Budd. 'You see, when this feller Craig was killed, a picture that he'd just bought was stolen.

That picture, which I've got 'ere' — he touched the parcel under his arm — 'was found last night beside the body of the man who was murdered in the Dark House. The paintin' is of a woman, an' I think you might recognise 'er.'

He took the picture from under his arm, and slipped off the wrapper. Charles Fairfax stared at it; and staring, his face changed. He opened his mouth in an attempt to speak, but it was only at the third effort that any coherent words came, and then they were almost inaudible.

'Beryl,' he mumbled. 'Yes, it's Beryl.'

'You recognise the lady?' murmured Mr. Budd.

By an effort Fairfax regained his composure.

'Yes,' he replied quietly. 'That is a portrait of my sister, Mrs. Grant.'

'Can you tell us who painted this picture?' asked the stout man.

The dark eyes clouded.

'Not for certain I can't,' said Charles Fairfax, 'but I should imagine that it was painted by Amos Grant.'

'Ah yes,' said Mr. Budd thoughtfully. 'Grant was an artist, wasn't 'e?'

'I suppose you've heard the story,' said Fairfax, and when the stout man nodded: 'Well, then, you must have heard that Grant lived in Paris before he came into his money. He was studying art over there. I believe he designed a lot of the scenery for the Folies Bergere revue.'

'Did he now?' murmured Mr. Budd. 'Well, well.'

He shot a sidelong glance at Inspector Haslett, but that individual's face was stolid. There was no doubt now that there was a connection between Lionel Craig's murder and Amos Grant.

'I don't want to bring up an unpleasant subject, Mr. Fairfax,' continued Mr. Budd, 'but have you seen or heard anythin' of your sister since she went away?'

There was an uncomfortable silence. Fairfax's fingers went to his mouth, and his jaw moved jerkily.

'I don't see how these questions can help you,' he said at length. 'What has my sister got to do with the death of these men?'

'Maybe nothin',' answered the stout superintendent. 'But we've got to foller up anythin' that may have a bearin'.'

'Well,' said Fairfax shortly, 'I haven't seen my sister since she left Grant. She wrote me a letter shortly after, and that is all I've ever heard of her.'

'Do you 'appen to have got this letter?' asked Mr. Budd.

For answer, Fairfax went over to the writing table and unlocked a drawer. Searching among its contents, he presently came back with an envelope, and in silence held it out. Mr. Budd took it and pulled out the folded sheet. The paper was cheap, the address a small street near Kennington Oval. He read the letter thoughtfully:

*Dear Chass,*

*I have written to father, but got no answer. But we were always pals, and I'm expecting better treatment from you. I know I've been a fool, according to the family, but I don't regret what I have done one little bit. Amos was impossible from the start, and, I think, a little mad. I hope that he will be sensible about this and divorce me as soon as possible, so that I can marry Frank. What I want you to do, Chass dear, is to lend me fifty pounds. I'll let you have it back as soon as Frank gets another job or I am well enough to get one. Frank does not know that I am writing to you — he would be furious if he did — and I wouldn't ask you for anything for myself or for him. But I think that Amos's child should come into the world under better conditions than I can give it at the moment. I'm relying on you, Chass. Don't let me down,*

*Yours ever,*

*Beryl.'*

Charles Fairfax, his hands clenched at his sides, watched the big man as he finished reading.

'Well,' he demanded harshly, 'are you satisfied?'

'Is this the only letter you received from your sister?' asked Mr. Budd.

'Yes,' said Fairfax, 'that is the only one.

As I didn't answer it she never wrote again.'

Mr. Budd's sleepy eyes opened suddenly very wide.

'You didn't answer this?' he said softly, but there was something in his tone that made the other wince.

'No,' he said roughly; 'and to this day I have never forgiven myself.'

There was agony in the dark eyes. This man, who had failed his sister in her time of need, had suffered for that failure — was suffering still — and the hardness that had crept into Mr. Budd's voice was absent when he spoke again.

'Did you ever make any effort to trace your sister?' he asked.

'I have made every effort,' said Fairfax. He took the letter from the other's podgy hand, and put it back in the envelope. 'But I left it too late. Inquiries at the address that she gives here showed that she had left. From there all trace of her was lost.'

'And the child?' said the big man gently.

'The child was born. It was a girl,' said Fairfax.

'The landlady at the Kennington lodging house told me that. That was all she could tell me,' he added bitterly.

'All this doesn't help us very much,' muttered Haslett uneasily. The atmosphere of tragedy that filled the air of this house, that showed in the face and every gesture of the man they were interviewing, was affecting even his stolid character. He was anxious to get away.

'I told you at the beginning,' said Fairfax, 'that I couldn't help you.'

'What I was hopin',' remarked Mr. Budd, 'was that you would be able to suggest how this painting of your sister comes to be mixed up in this business.'

'Well, I can't,' said the other. 'All I can say is that I'm pretty sure Amos painted it. You can see that it was painted by someone who hated her.' He looked at the picture and shuddered. 'The likeness is there, but it has been twisted to a vile caricature.'

They left him, a morose and worried man to pace once more up and down the shabby room.

# 8

## The Night Prowler

The chief topic of conversation at lunch
that day was, naturally, Craig's death, the
picture, and the dead man at the Dark
House. Both Driscoll and his son had
theories to express, and these they ex-
pounded at length.

Mr. Budd, however, remained silent.
He was not yet prepared to discuss the
matter. Only one remark — made by
the elder Driscoll — brought any sign of
interest from him. It was quite a casual
one, and referred to Beryl Grant.

' . . . It runs in the family,' the old man
was saying. 'Charles has got it, and his
father had it, too. Being the little finger of
the left hand it's scarcely noticeable, but
poor Beryl was very sensitive about it.
Instead of the usual two joints there's
only one.'

'That's interestin',' remarked the big

78

man. 'Have all the Fairfaxes got it?'

Driscoll nodded.

'Yes. What do they call it? Brachydactylous — that's it. It's not very common.'

The subject was changed, and they went on with their conjectures regarding the murders. When lunch was over, Mr. Budd went up to his room, and, lighting a cigar, lay down on the bed. He wanted to think, but the segments of the problem that were scattered in his mind refused to take coherent shape. Vaguely he saw little bits of it, but never the whole. The trouble was he had so little to go on. That remark of Driscoll's at lunch had given him further food for thought, but so far as the solution of the mystery went — the secret of the picture and who had killed Craig and the unknown man in the Dark House — it didn't help him.

He got up from his rest no wiser, and feeling — as he always did on these occasions — rather irritable.

The rest of the day passed without event of any sort. Dinner was a repetition of lunch, and afterwards the elder Driscoll retired to his study to work, while his son and Leek played snooker in the billiards room.

Mr. Budd sat smoking black cigars and thinking, and quite early took himself off to bed. He had put the picture of the Leering Lady on the mantelpiece in his room, and for a long time before he undressed he stood and stared at it, as though by the very intensity of his gaze he would force it to give up its secret. The vague idea — strengthened since the interview with Charles Fairfax — that was at the back of his mind was still stirring. Was it the right one? The picture offered no confirmation.

He gave it up at last, and wearily began to undress.

Ten minutes after he was in bed he was asleep, but not soundly, as was his wont. Into his dreams came a gigantic reproduction of the woman with the leering smile; and behind her, shadowy, scarcely seen, and utterly unreal, hovered the phantom shapes of Lionel Craig and the dead man at the Dark House.

As the lights went out one by one in Monk's Park, and nothing but the black bulk of the house remained silhouetted against the frozen blue of the sky, the man who had been watching, crouched in the shadow of the shrubbery, moved his cramped limbs, and uttered a sigh of relief. His hour's vigil had seemed endless. He was cold to the bone in spite of the heavy coat he wore, and his feet and hands were numb.

He glanced at the luminous dial of the watch on his wrist. Eleven-thirty. He would have to wait for another hour yet. It would be safer to let the people of the house get well asleep before he made a move.

He had already marked the window of the room that was his objective. He had seen the stout figure of Mr. Budd appear for a moment as he pulled the curtains. In his mind he had worked out a plan of the house, and he was fairly certain that he would be able to find the room without difficulty, once he succeeded in getting in. The french windows would be the best for that. The hasp was almost sure to be flimsy, and he had with him a strong knife.

There was little doubt that the picture would be in the detective's room — he wouldn't leave it about. If it hadn't been for that infernal bad luck at the Dark House on the previous night there would have been no need for all this trouble.

Well, nothing worth having was got without trouble, and the thing he was after was certainly worth having. Ease and luxury for the rest of his life! No more worry, no more staving off creditors. Peace of mind, comfort, opulence even. It was true that two — no three — men had had to die to make this possible. But what did that matter so long as nobody could prove that he had killed them? After all, in the old days — the good old days, as everyone was so fond of calling them — men had been killed for less.

It was infernally cold waiting. It had been stupid to come so early. If he had waited another hour and a half this hanging about in the snow would have been avoided. It was remarkable how slowly the time went when you were waiting — particularly when you were waiting in discomfort. The night was very still. The sound of shunting trucks came plainly from Midchester Junction, and from somewhere much farther off the faint, long-drawn wail of a locomotive's whistle.

Slowly the time passed. Midnight boomed out from the Town hall clock, and then after an eternity the half-hour. That freezing vigil was at an end.

The watcher moved cautiously towards the house.

Now was the moment of danger. He had to cross the snow-covered lawn. Should anyone be looking out from those sightless windows he would be plainly visible against the white, for there was no cover. But there was no one to see. Everybody in that house was sleeping.

He reached the window he had selected, and took out his knife. The blade was slipped between the sashes and the hasp yielded. A second later he was inside the house.

Before going any further he took a dark handkerchief from his pocket, and tied it round his nose and mouth.

Opening the door of the room in which

he found himself, the burglar made his way into the hall. To his right the staircase loomed, twisting up into the darkness above. Testing each stair before he put his full weight upon it, he went up. His objective was the first landing, and he reached it without making a sound. The room he wanted was, he calculated, the second door along the left-hand corridor, and towards this he went on tiptoe. At the door he stooped so that his ear was near the keyhole. Faintly from within came the sound of deep, regular breathing. The intruder tried the handle and pushed gently. With an inward sigh of relief he found that the door was unlocked.

He slipped noiselessly into the room and stood motionless in the darkness. So far so good. But the greatest risk had yet to be taken. His hand went to his pocket and came out grasping a torch. A dim ray of light broke up the blackness as he pressed the button — dim because he had taken the precaution to use an old battery that was nearly exhausted. The light flickered hither and thither and settled on the mantelpiece, bathing the picture of the Leering Lady in a soft radiance. Then it went out and the man who held the torch moved forward swiftly. His right hand went up and out and gripped the picture . . .

There was a slight click behind him, and his shadow, huge and distorted, leapt to life in the centre of a circle of blazing light. Dropping the picture, he swung round with a startled oath, blinking into the glare of the torch held in the hand of the man he had thought to be sleeping soundly in bed! The bed creaked as he sprang for the door and flew into the corridor. He heard a shout as he raced for the staircase, and as he reached the hall, the banging of doors and excited voices. But he was away, through the drawing room and out of the window by which he had entered. He tore a panting streak of blackness across the rectangle of the lawn, and the darkness of the shrubbery and the night swallowed him up.

# 9

## The Clue

The stage of the Theatre Royal at Midchester presented a spectacle of chaotic activity. Little groups of men, shirt-sleeved and perspiring, despite the cold, were hammering at long battens. Other little groups, similarly attired and equally hot, were busy fixing spot lights and replacing electric globes.

From the grid hung long ropes, snaking up into the darkness and waiting to carry up into the dusty flies the dozen or so cloths that had just arrived from the paint room and lay at the back of the stage rolled up. The noise of hammering and the shouting of men echoed through the theatre, for that afternoon at two o'clock would see the first dress rehearsal of Messrs. Harvey and MacLellon's Grand Spectacular Pantomime, *Beauty and the Beast*.

Fred Lane, the stage manager, a sheaf of papers in his hand, was here, there, and everywhere, superintending a hundred different jobs, and praying to Heaven that he had forgotten nothing.

'Up on yer long . . . Whoa! Centre now . . . That'll do, that'll do! Tie off!'

The raucous voice of the stage carpenter rose above the din of the hammers, and a huge sheet of painted canvas went sailing slowly and majestically upwards, to vanish in the gloom of the grid.

Roger Derwent, in hat and coat, strolled on to the stage from the direction of the stage door, and nodded to the harassed Fred Lane.

'How're things going?' he asked. 'Think you'll be ready to start at two?'

'On the tick,' was the answer. 'Hi! Electrics! Don't forget those three amber spots — No. 1 Batten! Yes, we shan't be late.'

'Good,' said Derwent. 'The sooner we start the sooner we'll get it over! Good morning, Mr. Hope.'

'Morning, Derwent.' Mr. Oswald Hope,

husky-voiced and fussy, came hurrying towards them. 'Fred, did you remember about those lamps for the change scene?'

'They're doing 'em now,' answered the stage manager. 'There's only another dozen to finish.'

'That's fine!' Mr. Hope nodded several times, and sent little, darting glances all over the stage. 'Have they gilded those kitchen chairs for the Palace scene? Good! Well, let me know when you've set the first scene and I'll run through the lighting plot.' He nodded again and disappeared in the direction of the property room.

'Well, I won't hinder you,' said Derwent. 'I suppose if I get back at one it'll be time enough?'

'Yes,' said Lane absently, and: 'What are you doing with that border? Not there, man — on the third set of lines, I told you!'

Derwent strolled away towards the stage door. As he reached it a fat man appeared in the narrow entrance.

'Good morning, Superintendent,' greeted Roger as he recognised the newcomer.

'Good mornin', sir,' said Mr. Budd.

'You're the very feller I wanted to see.'

Derwent looked surprised.

'I want to talk to you about that mornin' when Mr. Craig bought that picture,' the big man went on.

'But I've already told you all I know about that,' said Derwent.

'Can you recollect if there was anyone hangin' about at the time?' persisted Mr. Budd.

'There were several people passing in the street,' said Roger, 'but I don't remember anyone hanging about.'

Mr. Budd looked disappointed.

'I wonder whether Miss Waring noticed anythin'?' he murmured.

'I'm pretty sure she didn't,' answered Derwent. 'If she had she would have said something about it. Anyway, she will be here directly — I'm meeting her — so you can ask her yourself.'

At that moment Mr. Hope joined them.

'Hello!' he said. 'How are you? Found out yet who killed poor Craig?'

Mr. Budd shook his head sadly.

'Not yet I'm afraid, sir,' he answered, and the producer clicked his teeth.

'Terrible business!' he said. 'Nice fellow, Craig! Don't want to see me do you? Terribly busy. Got a dress rehearsal today.'

'No, sir, I don't want to see you,' said Mr. Budd, and Hope edged past them towards the exit.

'I must go,' he said. 'Hope you get the fellow, anyway. By the way if you and your friends 'ud like to come and see the rehearsal, come along. Starts at two — sharp!'

He hurried away, and Mr. Budd waited talking to Roger Derwent until Joan Waring arrived. She listened gravely to his questions, but she could not add anything to Roger's statement.

Leaving the theatre, Mr. Budd made his way to the police station. Haslett had news when he arrived.

'There's been a message from the Yard,' he said. 'They've identified that fellow from the fingerprints. His name is — was — Hipple. He was a little sneak-thief and pickpocket, and he'd just finished a sentence of eighteen months for robbery with violence.'

'Good,' said Mr. Budd. 'So that's him, eh?'

After a chat with Haslett he went back to Monk's Park. During lunch he suggested that they might like to take advantage of Mr. Hope's offer and see the dress rehearsal of the pantomime, a suggestion that they all hailed with delight.

The show had started when they got there. Mr. Harvey, of Messrs. Harvey and MacLellon, had come from London, and sat beside Mr. Oswald Hope, and there were other little scattered groups in the stalls; but for the most part the theatre still remained swathed in its dustsheets. Mr. Budd was given a seat in the third row, with Leek on one side of him and the Driscolls on the other.

The pantomime was the usual thing — a little better than most provincial shows, perhaps, but still conforming to type. Bright colours, pretty costumes, popular songs, and threadbare jokes; the whole galaxy which is epitomised in the word 'pantomime' ran its course.

Mr. Oswald Hope had done his work well. Only twice during the first part was the show stopped while he harangued the company over a slight hitch.

At last came the big scene — the finale of the first half. The Demon King, having tried to be as bad as he possibly could all through, and having been foiled by the Fairy Queen, played his trump card, and turns the Prince into a beast and his palace into a den in the mountains.

At one instant there was the palace, the next by a lighting trick, it had vanished, leaving a dim, greenly lit rocky cave. Leek and the Driscolls applauded as the curtain came down, and the scene deserved it. But Mr. Budd seemed to have suddenly been turned to stone. With dropping jaw and wide eyes he stared at the stage.

'Clever wasn't it?' said the lean sergeant, but his superior did not answer. With a grunt he hoisted himself out of his seat and left the theatre without a word.

★   ★   ★

The big man made his way as quickly as he could into the town. At the post office he consulted a local directory, and then, finding a cab, was driven to Monk's Park. He kept the cab waiting and returned after a few minutes with the picture of the Leering Lady under his arm. He was taken to an address that he had noted in the directory, and an hour later returned to the theatre.

The rehearsal was over when he entered the stage door, and the Driscolls, who with Leek were talking to Mr. Hope, greeted his appearance with surprise.

'What in the world made you dash away like that?' asked the elder Driscoll.

'I suddenly remembered somethin' that I 'ad to do,' replied Mr. Budd. 'Everythin' go off all right sir?'

Mr. Hope, to whom the question was addressed, expressed his complete satisfaction, and they all stood chatting, eventually being joined by Joan Waring and Roger Derwent. Mr. Budd laid down the picture, which he carried under his arm and produced one of his cigars. He apparently forgot all about it, for when they at last left the theatre he was carrying nothing.

They were halfway to Monk's Park when Leek drew attention to this fact.

'Didn't you 'ave a parcel under your

arm when you come back?' he said.

'Why yes I did, now you come ter mention it,' grunted Mr. Budd. 'Must 'ave left it at the theatre. Stupid thin' to do.'

Something in his tone warned the sergeant not to pursue the subject, and he relapsed into silence.

Haslett called to see Mr. Budd during the evening, and the hospitable Driscoll insisted on his staying to dinner. It was in the middle of the meal that the stout superintendent dropped his bombshell. Abruptly and with no reference to the conversation that had gone before, he suddenly turned to the elder Driscoll.

'How far is it from here to the churchyard?' he asked.

For a moment there was silence while the man to whom the question had been addressed recovered from his surprise.

'It all depends which churchyard you mean,' he answered at length, 'The new churchyard is at the other end of the town, but the old one — '

'Which one contains the family vault of the Grants?' interrupted Mr. Budd.

'The old one,' said Driscoll, raising his eyebrows.

'Then that's the one I mean,' replied the big man calmly.

'Well, that's close to the Dark House,' explained Driscoll. 'In fact, the wall forms a boundary to the estate.'

He waited, evidently expecting some explanation, but Mr. Budd went on eating.

'What's the idea?' asked Haslett with a touch of irritation in his voice. 'Why did you ask how far the churchyard is?'

'Because we're goin' there as soon as we've 'ad dinner,' answered Mr. Budd. 'You an' I an' Leek.'

'We're — what?' Haslett almost shouted in his surprise.

'You 'eard what I said,' murmured the fat detective.

'Why are we going to the churchyard?' demanded the inspector.

'Because,' said Mr. Budd, 'the murderer of Lionel Craig 'ull be there some time durin' the night, an' I'd like you to meet 'im.'

# 10

## The Man Who Came in the Night

The night was dark — very dark indeed, for there was no moon, and heavy, snow-laden clouds obscured the sky. The wind, which had come with the darkness, was from the north and blew in fitful gusts — an icy wind that cut through to the bone and chilled the blood. In spite of the heavy coats they wore the three were shivering.

Mr. Budd led the way along the old post road, with Haslett and Leek at his heels. With the exception of the stout man, none of them knew what the night held in store; for Mr. Budd was in one of his most secretive moods, and refused to explain himself.

'Just you do what I tell you,' he said in reply to their questions, 'and maybe you'll see what you'll see.'

Haslett was a little annoyed at this

high-handed method, but the melancholy Leek was used to it, and accepted the situation philosophically.

They passed the dark opening to the drive that led up to the deserted house in which Amos Grant had breathed his last, and the little bag-snatcher had been done to death, and on along the road to the rickety gate which gave access to the churchyard. The ruins of the old church showed up blackly against the snow which lay thickly on the branches of the giant trees that clustered round them; and from the powdery whiteness of the ground protruded the crumbling head-stones that marked the graves of people whose bones were by now almost as white as the blanket that lay above them.

'We'll have ter be careful 'ere,' whispered Mr. Budd as he led them past the gate and along by the low wall. 'I don't want our footsteps ter show in the snow.'

He selected a convenient spot and laboriously climbed over, signing to the other two to do the same.

Near the wall there was a sheltered strip, where the snow lay only thinly, and on which they could walk in single file without leaving very discernible traces. The big man followed this for about a hundred yards, and then struck off across the open ground, picking his way delicately between the gravestones.

It was very still here among the forgotten dead. Except for the creaking of the branches as the breeze swept through the trees, and the muffled thud of falling snow as it thawed, no sound disturbed the serenity of the place.

The stout superintendent was making for a dark, oblong structure, that, as they drew nearer, Leek saw was a small, flat-roofed building. Reaching it, Mr. Budd stopped. His hand went to his pocket and a soft splash of light fell on the granite wall.

'The fam'ly tomb of the Grants,' he announced.

'Very interesting!' grunted Haslett sarcastically. 'Have you brought us all this way in this infernal cold to show us that?'

'No, to show you somethin' else,' retorted Mr. Budd. He stooped and felt about in the snow at one end of the tomb.

There was a moment's silence and then a grinding, creaking sound. Haslett uttered a gasp that was echoed by Leek as part of the end of the vault swung upwards, revealing a dark opening.

'There should be some steps,' muttered Mr. Budd, shining his light. ''Ere we are! Now careful!'

He began to descend gingerly, and the other two followed. The steps led down into musty-smelling darkness, heavy, fetid darkness, reeking of decay.

'Squeeze past me,' murmured Mr. Budd. 'I've got ter close the stone.'

They obeyed. The thud of the stone dropping back reached them, and then the light of the torch cut a cone-shaped ray through the velvety darkness. They were in a narrow, oblong chamber barely four feet wide, but nearly a dozen feet long and of a height that just enabled them to stand upright in comfort; a long, passage-like chamber, paved with stone and enclosed by walls of slimy brickwork. It was fitted with massive stone shelves, and on these rested coffins in varying stages of decay, and one that was, in comparison, almost new.

Mr. Budd touched it lightly.

'Amos Grant's,' he said, and his voice sounded queerly muffled in that confined space.

'Why have you brought us here?' asked Haslett.

'Because the man we're after 'ull come here,' answered the stout superintendent soberly. 'The man who has killed three times.'

'You mean twice, don't yer?' said Leek. 'Craig an' that feller Hipple . . . '

'And Snellkins,' snapped Mr. Budd. 'It's my opinion that that old man never left the Dark House on the night his master died!'

'Good God!' Haslett stared at him in the feeble torchlight. 'You mean that he was murdered?'

'I mean just that,' agreed Mr. Budd. 'An' if you want to meet his murderer I'll 'ave to put out this light. I don't know when 'e'll come, but I hope we shan't 'ave to wait 'ere too long.'

They waited in silence and darkness, and it was one of the longest waits that

Leek could remember. The stillness inside the vault was like the stillness of some cavern deep in the heart of a mountain. None of the ordinary night sounds could penetrate those thick walls. They might have been entombed in the Great Pyramid.

But at last came a sound — the faintest possible sound, like a mouse scratching at the wainscot — and Mr. Budd stiffened. The sound came again, this time more definite. There was a grinding noise and a spark of light appeared at the end of the vault. It lengthened rapidly into a long, narrow rod. Somebody with a torch had opened the way in at the top of the steps.

The light grew brighter, and a man appeared at the head of the steps. At first he was no more than a dim smudge, but as he came slowly down the reflected light showed him up more clearly. He was of medium height and carried a torch and a bag, but his face was invisible behind the glare. He moved cautiously forward sweeping his light before him. Another yard and that fan-shaped ray would strike full upon the watchers crouched against the wall. But before that yard could be taken, Mr. Budd hurled himself bodily upon the intruder and bore him backwards to the ground. The light went out as the torch fell and broke. But the darkness only lasted for a moment. From Inspector Haslett's hand sprang a broad sword blade of light that focused on the struggling men, and then Leek went to the assistance of his superior, and the man who had come in the night was rendered helpless.

'Who is he?' grunted Haslett, and turned his torch on the man's face. And then he gasped, for the distorted face that looked back at him was the face of Roger Derwent!

# 11

## A Question of Light

'What I'm goin' ter tell you now,' said Mr. Budd, comfortably ensconced in a deep armchair in the library at Monk's Park, 'is the finished version of this affair. This feller Derwent — or Roger Snellkins, which is his real name — 'as made a statement an' filled in the gaps.' He blew a cloud of smoke from between his thick lips. 'The story of the Leerin' Lady,' he continued, 'begins on the night two years ago, when Amos Grant died. He'd been a bit mad for years, an' the special form 'is madness took was that 'is wife shouldn't get any of his money at his death. He converted all he had into cash, an' hid it in the fam'ly vault — in one of the coffins where we found it today. Even 'is old servant, Snellkins, didn't know what 'e'd done with it. Then he painted that picture of his wife an' incorporated in it the secret of the hidin' place.'

'How did he manage that?' asked the elder Driscoll.

'I'll come to that presently,' said Mr. Budd. 'It was quite simple once you got the hang of it. When Grant 'ad his heart attack it wasn't fatal at once. An' while he lay ill he sort o' changed. His 'atred of his wife was replaced by a desire to make 'er some sort o' restitution. Maybe durin' those two hours before his death he became sane. However, he took old Snellkins, who 'e knew 'e could trust, into his confidence about the money, an' told 'im the secret of the paintin'. He made 'im promise that he would find Beryl Grant an' give 'er the picture with the instructions for findin' the money. He didn't tell even the old man where he had put that. And then he died.

'Snellkins was just goin' to Midchester to get a doctor — Grant wouldn't let 'im while 'e was livin' — when young Roger Snellkins turned up. He was the old man's nephew, and a bit of a black sheep. He was down an' out, an' had spent his last few shillin's to get to 'is uncle, hoping that he would 'elp him as he had before.

The old man was pleased to see 'im. He was frightened an' worried, an' he was glad of somebody to help 'im. He told Roger the story of the picture, an' Roger, of course, suggested at once that they should collar the money for themselves. Three hundred an' fifty thousand pounds for the taking, an' no one any the wiser. All they had to do was to put the picture through the process, which Grant had explained, find the hidin' place o' the money an' keep their mouths shut. Old Snellkins was horrified at the suggestion, an' refused to have anythin' to do with it.

'Well, ter cut a long story short, Roger killed the old man, an' buried the body in the garden, clearin' off with the picture. He'd as good as got the money, for 'e only wanted a little while in private with that paintin' ter know where it was hid. But fate, in the person of Hipple, took a hand in the game. Roger had packed the picture in 'is suitcase, an' when he left the Dark House he went to the station, intendin' to leave the bag in the cloak-room while 'e found a lodgin'. He put it down for a moment while he made an inquiry, an' durin' that moment Hipple came along an' pinched it!

'The followin' day Hipple was arrested fer pickin' pockets, and as an old offender got eighteen months. The bag and its contents was left with 'is brother-in-law, a respectable, 'ard workin' plumber, with whom 'e'd bin boardin', an' who, thinkin' the bag was Hipple's property, kept it for 'im until 'e came out. In the meanwhile, Roger, unable to lay 'is hands on the money without the picture, went back to actin', which was his job, an' pottered about round the provinces until at length he was engaged to play in the pantomime at the Theatre Royal.

'Just about this time, Hipple comes out o' prison, collects the bag from 'is brother-in-law's, an', bein' 'ard up, sells the lot to various places, finally sellin' the picture to Silas Mann, where it was seen by Craig. Derwent recognised it at once, but was afraid to say anything, because he didn't know how much was known about it. Even after two years it might connect him with the Dark House an' what lay buried there, an' he didn't want that. But he made up 'is mind to 'ave the picture. As soon as he had got rid of Miss Warin', he went back to the theatre an' made 'imself up as unlike 'imself as he could. There was nobody at the theatre, so he could slip in and out without bein' seen. He had very little money, but he offered to buy the picture at first from Craig. Craig, however, bein' a collector, wouldn't listen, an' then a fatal thin' happened. Craig recognised Derwent, an' taxed 'im with tryin' to play a practical joke on 'im. In a fit of panic, Derwent stabbed 'im and ran off with the picture. He knew that there would be an immediate hue an' cry about it, an' that if it was seen in his possession, nothin' could save 'im from 'angin'. An' then he thought of the Dark House. Nobody ever went near the place, an' he could leave the picture there with safety. He did so, removed his make up, an' was just in time to reach the theatre for the afternoon's rehearsal. Later that night 'e went back to the Dark House, an' to his surprise found Hipple bendin' over the picture an' lookin' at it in the light of a candle. Hipple — Derwent, of course, hadn't the faintest idea who he was — penniless, footsore, an' weary, had chosen the Dark House to snatch a night's rest. He had nowhere else to go, for his relative wouldn't have him. But if Derwent didn't know Hipple, 'e knew Derwent. He had seen 'im in the town an' knew of his job at the theatre, an' hopin' to make a little money by blackmail, 'e taxed him with the murder of Craig. Derwent 'ad to kill him then to save 'is skin, an' he'd done it when I got there. That's about all, I think, except the picture. That was clever, but simple, an' I wouldn't 'ave stumbled on the idea if I hadn't gone to that dress rehearsal at the theatre. Do you remember the vanishin' o' the palace an' a cave takin' its place? It was all done by lightin'. They paint one scene entirely in red an' orange an' pink an' yellow, an' they paint another on the top of it in green an' blue, etc. When the scene is flooded with red light you can only see the one that's painted in green, an' when it's flooded with green light you can only see the one that's painted in red, etc. I took that picture to a scenic artist in the town an' suggested that somethin' of the sort had been done there. He tried it an' I was right. In a red light the face of the woman vanished, an' you could see a picture of the churchyard an' a tomb. There was some very small writin' givin' instructions for enterin' the tomb an' findin' the hidin' place of the money. Grant understood this lightin' business, because 'e used to design scenery for the Folies Bergere revues in Paris . . . '

'That's what Hipple's dying words meant, then?' said Driscoll, and Mr. Budd nodded.

'Derwent had brought a red electric lamp with him for use on the picture,' he said.

'How did you know that Derwent was the man?' bellowed young Driscoll.

The big man smiled.

'I didn't,' he replied. 'Not until he entered that tomb. But I knew it was somebody from the theatre. The night he broke in for the picture he left a smear of greasepaint on the mantelpiece. I left the picture at the theatre, guessin' that whoever it was behind the business wouldn't be able to resist the temptation of coming after the money at once.'

'How much money was there?'

'Nearly three hundred thousand pounds,' answered Mr. Budd.

'And all that goes to the State,' sighed the younger Driscoll.

'It don't do nothin' of the kind,' corrected the stout superintendent. 'It goes to Amos Grant's daughter.'

'If you can find her,' grunted old Driscoll.

'I 'ave found her,' replied Mr. Budd calmly. 'She's in Midchester at this moment. She inherited a love of the theatre from Carstairs, the man she was always taught to believe was her father, an' from her mother, she inherited the Fairfax finger. She's playin' Beauty in the pantomime at the Theatre Royal!'

'Joan Waring!' exclaimed Driscoll. 'Well, what a coincidence. It's like a book.'

'It's my experience, sir,' remarked Mr. Budd thoughtfully, 'that there are more coincidences in real life than ever appear in books. Or perhaps they ain't altogether coincidences. Maybe there's a plan somewhere that sees to these thin's. You can't really tell.'

# 2

# The Seven Sleeping Men

# 1

## The Puzzle of the Playing Cards

One of the strangest, and certainly the most mysterious affairs, which that stout and sleepy looking man, Superintendent Robert Budd, had ever been connected with began very prosaically in the saloon bar of a small public house in Streatham. The big man lived in a neat little villa within a few minutes' walk of the Red Lion, and, when the exigencies of his profession permitted, was in the habit of dropping in after his supper for a tankard of beer and a chat with such acquaintances as he might find there. The principal topic of conversation on these occasions was the growing of roses, which was Mr. Budd's particular hobby, and much argument would ensue concerning the relative values of fertilisers, and the proper steps to be taken when dealing with such annoyances as mildew and greenfly.

He came in earlier than usual one wet and stormy night, and, after shaking the water from his hat, walked ponderously over to the bar.

'Good evenin', sup'intendent!' greeted the landlord, reaching automatically for a tankard.

'Good evenin',' said Mr. Budd heavily, 'if yer can call it a good evenin'! It's rainin' hard enough ter float a battleship.'

'Bin rainin' all day,' said the landlord, with the air of a man who was imparting a piece of exclusive information. 'Queer weather for the time o' year, I call it.'

'That's mild fer what I call it!' grunted the big man, and picked up the beer which the landlord had drawn. 'It don't seem to matter what time o' the year it is these days. It rains jest the same.'

He took a deep draught from the tankard, and set it down.

'Ah, that's better!' he remarked, smacking his lips appreciatively.

'There's nothin' like a drop o' beer,' agreed the landlord.

'Except two drops o' beer!' said Mr. Budd, and glanced round the bar to see if there was anyone there he knew.

It held only a smattering of people as yet, and although they were mostly familiar by sight, there was none of his particular cronies. He emptied the remainder of his tankard, called for it to be refilled, and, lighting one of his thin, black cigars, carried the beer over to a small table in a corner and sat down.

A rather weedy little man who had been standing at the bar alone, gloomily sipping a whisky-and-soda, shot a covert glance at him, hesitated nervously, and, finally making up his mind, picked up his glass and came over to the table.

'Excuse me, sir,' he said diffidently, 'but you are connected with the police, aren't you?'

Mr. Budd nodded.

'I thought you were,' said the little man. 'I've seen you in here once or twice, and I was told you were. I wonder if I could ask your advice on a small matter which has caused me some concern?'

'Sit down,' said the big man good-naturedly. 'I'll do what I can. What's the trouble?'

The little man perched himself uncomfortably on the edge of the chair which Mr. Budd indicated.

'It's most kind of you,' he said gratefully. 'Let me start by introducing myself. My name is Pettegew — er — Mitchell Pettegew, and I have recently leased a house near Streatham Common; perhaps you know it — the — er — the Cedars?' He blinked at the big man inquiringly through his pince-nez; but Mr. Budd shook his head. 'You don't?' he went on rapidly. 'It's really of no consequence. I — I only mentioned it because the address may have something to do with this — well, I hardly know what to call it — persecution is too strong a word.'

'Has somebody been annoyin' you, Mr. Pettegew?' asked the stout superintendent.

'Well, no — er — not exactly,' stammered Mr. Pettegew. 'The whole thing is really very mysterious and — and — inexplicable. You see, I have no idea where these playing cards come from, or what they mean.'

116

'Playin' cards?' echoed Mr. Budd in astonishment, and the little man nodded rapidly.

'An ordinary playing card, with two or three words pencilled on the back, and enclosed in a plain envelope!' he said. 'One has come every morning by the first post for the past week. It really is most extraordinary!'

Mr. Budd thought, privately, that it wasn't extraordinary at all. Somebody was evidently playing a practical joke on this timid little man.

'What does it say on 'em?' he asked. 'These words on the backs?'

'I have the cards here — in my wallet,' replied Mr. Pettegew, fumbling in his breast pocket. 'There are seven of them.'

He produced a worn leather pocket-book and from amongst its numerous contents extracted seven playing cards, which he handed to the fat detective. Mr. Budd took them, expecting the usual obscene messages, which is the general stock-in-trade of the anonymous sender of such things, but a glance showed him that in this case he was mistaken. The cards had evidently all been taken from the same pack, and each bore on its back several words scribbled in pencil. The fat man spread them fanwise in his podgy fingers, and read the inscriptions, his forehead puckered in a frown.

'In red ebony.' 'To the seven sleepers.' 'Box to the Sin-Eater.' 'Aeolian harp murmurs.' 'Bring dragonfly.' 'Of the Sphinx an.' 'By the shadow.'

His frown deepened, and he rubbed his fleshy chin in perplexity.

'This looks a lot o' rubbish ter me,' he grunted. 'What's a Sin-Eater, when it's at home?'

'A Sin-Eater,' said Mr. Pettegew informatively, 'was a man in the olden days who used to attend funerals for the purpose of eating bread and drinking ale that was placed on the coffin of the corpse. It was thought that he thus took upon himself all the sins of the — er — deceased, who would thereby be saved from eternal damnation.'

'H'm!' remarked the fat detective. 'Well, that's a new one on me! I s'pose it didn't matter about this sin-eatin' feller bein' damned — he was getting' paid fer it?' He began to lay the cards down on the table in front of him, one by one, as though he were going to play patience. 'That makes a little more sense, but not much,' he murmured, almost to himself, and Mr. Pettegew leaned forward.

'What have you found?' he asked eagerly.

'I've put the cards in the order of their value,' replied the big man. 'They run from an ace to a seven. I don't think it makes thin's much clearer, though. The message, if yer can call such a lot o' gibberish a message, now runs: 'Bring dragonfly in red ebony box to the Sin-Eater by the shadow of the Sphinx an aeolian harp murmurs to the seven sleepers'!'

'Extraordinary!' exclaimed Mr. Pettegew. 'Remarkable! What can it possibly mean?'

Mr. Budd shook his head.

'It don't mean anythin' ter me!' he declared. 'I s'pose you don't know nothin' about a red ebony box or a dragonfly?'

'Nothing whatever!' declared the little man emphatically. 'So far as I am concerned, the whole thing is a complete and utter enigma. What would you advise me to do about it?'

'Nothin',' said Mr. Budd, without hesitation. 'It's either a joke, or a mistake. How long have you been livin' at yer present address?'

'For just over a month,' replied Mr. Pettegew.

'Then maybe these was intended for the previous tenant,' suggested the stout superintendent.

'That is not possible,' said the other, shaking his head. 'The envelopes were addressed to me in person. There could be no question of a mistake.'

'H'm, interestin' an perculiar,' muttered Mr. Budd, screwing up his large face thoughtfully. 'Seems a silly sort o' joke fer anyone ter play, unless it's some kids who've been readin' these 'ere mystery stories. The writin' isn't kids' writin', though.' He lifted his tankard and drained the rest of his beer. 'I don't see what you can do,' he went on, 'except ignore the 'ole thin'.'

'Thank you,' said Mr. Pettegew gratefully. 'It was all so strange and perplexing that I felt I had to get advice, and you appeared to be the right person to ask. May I' — he hesitated nervously — 'may I offer you a little refreshment? I — er — '

'Thank you very much,' said Mr. Budd; 'I'll 'ave a pint o' bitter, if you please.'

Mr. Pettegew went over to the bar, and the big man took out a notebook and, more from habit than anything else, scribbled down the message of the playing cards. Later, he was to be glad he had done so, for the nervous little man never reached his house near Streatham Common that night. A patrolling policeman found his body lying near the entrance to the short drive; the knife that had killed him still protruding from between his narrow shoulder blades. Every pocket had been turned inside out, and the wallet, in which Mr. Budd had seen him put the seven playing cards before he left the Red Lion, was gone.

# 2

## The Girl with the Silver Hair

'I can't make head or tail of it,' grunted Mr. Budd, wearily, leaning back in the padded chair behind his desk. 'It's jest a jumble o' nonsense, that's what it is.'

Sergeant Leek, perched uncomfortably on the only other chair in the cheerless office, looked across at him with his usual expression of mournful resignation.

'I expect it 'ud be clear, if yer knew what it was about,' he said helpfully.

Mr. Budd gave him a withering glance.

'That's a brilliant remark, that is!' he growled. ''Ow long did it take yer to think that out?'

'Well, it's true, ain't it?' said Leek in a slightly aggrieved tone. 'What I mean is, you can't understand the message because yer don't know what the person what wrote it is gettin' at — '

'Tell me somethin' I don't know!'

snapped the big man irritably. 'Everythin' you've just said was obvious!'

The lean sergeant sighed, and Mr. Budd closed his eyes and relapsed into silence. He had just come back from a long and unprofitable investigation at Streatham, and he was both tired and disgruntled. The news of the murder of the unfortunate Pettegew had reached him on his arrival at the Yard that morning, and he had immediately notified the Assistant Commissioner of his meeting with the dead man on the previous night, and all that had transpired. The result, as he had expected, was that he had been put in charge of the case, and a pretty difficult business it looked like being.

There was no clue whatever to the identity of the murderer, except that the crime had evidently been committed for the sole purpose of gaining possession of the playing cards. This was proved by the fact that, although the pockets had all been turned out, only the wallet had been taken. The rest of the dead man's belongings, including the other contents of the wallet, had been left strewn about the ground where he lay.

Such meagre information as he had been able to glean about Pettegew himself threw no light at all on his death. He had been a bachelor, and although the Cedars was a fairly large house, had lived there alone except for a small staff of servants. Mr. Budd had interviewed these, but since they had only been engaged a month previously, they could tell him very little. It appeared, however, that Pettegew had come from abroad, where he had been in business, and this was borne out by the agent from whom he had leased the house. He had paid a year's rent in advance instead of the usual references, explaining that he had only recently arrived in England and knew nobody. The agent thought he had mentioned South Africa as the place whence he had come, but of this he couldn't be sure.

Was there a connection between this apparent mystery surrounding his previous existence and his death? thought Mr. Budd. It was difficult to believe it without also believing that he knew all about the playing cards, and this the big man could not credit. He was still cogitating over the puzzle, when there came a tap at the door and a messenger entered.

'This has just come for you, sir,' said the man, and laid an envelope on the desk.

Mr. Budd hoisted himself up in his chair with difficulty and picked up the envelope.

'Who brought it?' he asked, sliding a fat thumb under the flap.

'A shabby-looking boy, sir,' answered the messenger.

Mr. Budd drew out the contents of the envelope and uttered an exclamation as he saw that it was a playing card! Turning it over, he read the message scrawled in pencil across the face:

'If you wish to find the red ebony box, go to the ace of Great Oram Street tonight at nine.'

'What is it?' asked Leek curiously.

'More fantastic rubbish!' growled the big man disparagingly. 'I s'pose the boy who brought this has gone?' He turned to the waiting messenger. The man nodded.

'Yes, sir,' he said. 'He just left the note, and went away at once.'

'I'll bet he did!' said Mr. Budd, glowering at the card in his hand. 'All right, you can go, too.'

The messenger departed, and the stout superintendent read the pencilled scrawl again.

'What's the 'ace of Great Oram Street' mean?' he grunted. 'Why can't these people stick to plain English?'

'There's a Great Oram Street at Vauxhall,' said Leek informatively. ''P'raps that's where they mean?'

'Maybe,' muttered his superior, still staring at the card. 'I wonder why this was sent ter me? H'm! Interestin' an' perculiar.'

'Somebody wants yer to get this 'ere red ebony box,' said the sergeant brightly, and Mr. Budd heaved a weary sigh.

'I've gathered that,' he said patiently. 'It says so 'ere, so I deduce that's the idea. But who wants me ter find it, an' why?'

Since Leek could find no suggestion to

offer in answer to these questions, he remained discreetly silent.

'It's a curious thin',' murmured the big man, shaking his head sadly, 'but you never seem ter 'ave any new ideas. You come out with a mine of information that everybody else has known fer years. Yer'll be boundin' brightly into this office one day an' tellin' me that Queen Anne's dead!'

'And I'd be right!' said Leek, a statement which so flabbergasted Mr. Budd that he could think of no reply.

It was still raining heavily when he left the Yard, and set off with Leek to Great Oram Street, and the gloomy vicinity of Vauxhall looked even more uninviting than usual when they stepped out of the taxi on to the streaming pavements.

Mr. Budd had instructed the driver to stop at the top of the street, since he had no idea what, or where, the 'ace' mentioned in the message might be.

Great Oram Street turned out to be a short thoroughfare, lined by two rows of barrack-like grey houses, mainly given over to dingy lodgings, to judge by the notices displayed in the windows.

The big man walked slowly along one side of this dismal street, keeping a sharp lookout for anything that would tell him that he had reached his destination. But he saw nothing that could, even vaguely, be construed to resemble an 'ace'. With a disgusted grunt, he crossed the narrow roadway and tried the other side. Here he met with better luck. The first house at the end of the row was larger than the rest; a grim-looking building, silent and lifeless. The blistered front door bore the number 18 in discoloured paint, which had once been white, and beneath it had been pinned a single playing card — the ace of spades.

'This is us,' muttered Mr. Budd, eyeing the card sleepily. 'Though why in the world they couldn't 'ave just put the number in that message is beyond me. Let's see what happens next.'

He went up to the door and knocked sharply. After a short delay it was opened, and the dim figure of a woman appeared on the threshold.

'Good evenin',' said Mr. Budd pleasantly. 'Do you know anythin' about this?'

He produced the card he had received and held it out. She took it in silence, glanced at it in the dim light of a nearby street lamp, and standing aside, ushered them into the dark hall.

'If you will wait a moment,' she said in a low voice, 'I will get a light.'

She went silently away, leaving behind the faintest trace of an exotic perfume. They waited in complete darkness, and presently a glimmer of light heralded her return. She carried a candle in her hand, and by its uncertain flame the big man saw that she was a tall, slim girl, dressed in a smartly cut suit of some soft black material. She was very lovely, and at first glance he thought that her hair was unusually fair and then he discovered that it was silver.

'You have come for the box,' she said, and it was a statement rather than a question. 'Please come this way, and I will give it to you.'

She walked over to a door on the right of the passage-like hall, and held it open. From the quick glance that he had been able to take at the hall and the staircase,

Mr. Budd had come to the rather surprising conclusion that the house was an empty one, and now, as he entered the room into which the girl with the silver hair invited him, this conclusion was confirmed. The floor was bare and covered with dust; the walls were grimy; the fire grate choked with rubbish. There was no furniture of any kind, and the girl had to set the candle she carried on the mantelshelf before she picked up a square, red object, and held it out to the big man.

'This is what you came for,' she said simply.

It was a box made of red ebony, with a brass lock, and was roughly the size of a seven and sixpenny novel. The fat man examined it curiously, pressed a tiny catch above the brass lock, and found that it was not locked. Leek craned forward as Mr. Budd raised the lid and peered into the interior. The case was lined with black velvet, and on this sable background rested a life-size dragonfly, exquisitely fashioned of coloured glass. The wings, opal-hued, shone vividly in the candlelight, and were so finely spun that they quivered under the big man's breath.

'Pretty, ain't it?' said Leek admiringly.

'Very pretty,' agreed Mr. Budd, with a puzzled frown.

'What do you know about this, miss?'

'I know nothing about it,' replied the girl. 'I was merely told to give it to the person who would come here at nine.'

'Who told you?' asked the stout detective.

'The man who engaged me,' she answered. 'I don't know his name.'

Mr. Budd rubbed a large hand over his chin.

'Let's get this clear,' he said slowly. 'You was engaged by some man ter come 'ere, and hand this thin' over to somebody who would call at nine? Is that right?'

She nodded.

'How did this unknown man come to engage you?' inquired the detective, and she answered without hesitation.

'He called at my flat,' she said, 'he had got my name and address from my agents, and he offered me five pounds if I would come to this address and hand that box over to the person who would call for it. I thought it was a queer thing to ask, but I was out of work, and five pounds was five pounds.'

'I see,' murmured Mr. Budd, pulling gently at the lobe of his right ear. 'You an actress, miss?'

'I'm anything,' she replied, a trifle bitterly. 'A showgirl, a model, a film-extra — anything I can get. Is there something wrong?'

'Well, there is, an' there isn't,' replied the big man evasively. 'Will yer give me your name an' address, miss?'

'Jill Hope,' she answered, without hesitation, and mentioned a block of flats near Russell Square. 'I'm sure there is something wrong. You're a detective aren't you?'

'It seems ter be a matter of opinion!' said Mr. Budd sadly. 'Tell me some more about this man, miss. What was he like?'

But here the girl was vague. He wasn't very tall and he wasn't very short. Rather a nondescript individual, she thought.

'Sounds like almost anybody,' grunted

Mr. Budd disappointedly. 'An' did 'e give yer that card ter pin on the front door?'

'Yes,' she replied. 'He was most particular about that.'

'H'm,' muttered the fat detective. 'Interestin' an perculiar. I don't think I've ever come across such an extraordinary business. It's like somethin' out of a story.' He looked down at the box in his hand. 'This is a pretty little thin', but I don't know what use it is. Maybe — '

A sharp knock on the front door echoed through the house and stopped him.

'Who can that be?' whispered the girl, with a sudden frown.

'Go an' see, miss,' murmured Mr. Budd softly. 'P'raps it's the feller what engaged yer. If it is, cough, and we'll come out an' have a word with him.'

She hesitated for a second, and then went out into the hall. They heard her fumble at the latch of the front door, and then a voice harsh and slurred came to their ears.

'I've come for the red ebony box,' it said peremptorily 'Where is it?'

'Will you come in?' replied the low voice of the girl, and Mr. Budd noted that she had not given the pre-arranged signal.

There was a heavy tramp of feet on the bare boards of the passage, and a man loomed in the doorway. He uttered an exclamation as he caught sight of Mr. Budd and the thin sergeant, and the big man saw that a handkerchief covered his face from eyes to chin.

'Who are you?' he rasped sharply, and an automatic appeared with almost magical rapidity in his gloved hand. 'What are you doing with that box?'

'Who are *you*?' retorted Mr. Budd.

'I'm known as the Sin-Eater!' was the reply. 'Give me that box, or I'll fill your fat hide so full of lead that you'll fall down with the weight of it!'

# 3

## The Secret of the Glass Dragonfly

Mr. Budd looked sleepily at the man with the automatic, and beyond him to the terrified face of the girl hovering in the doorway.

'I'm glad yer didn't say 'put up yer hands',' he remarked approvingly. 'As a form of introduction that's gettin' rather monotonous. So you're the Sin-Eater, are yer? I should think you must 'ave eaten a hell of a lot o' sins in yer time!'

'Give me the box!' snapped the man. 'I'm in a hurry.'

He took a pace forward, and stopped with a muttered oath as a sound from the hall reached him.

'Now then,' called a voice gruffly, 'what's going on in there?' The clump of heavy steps thudded along the passage, and as the masked man swung round a police-man appeared in the doorway. Sergeant

Leek, taking advantage of the fact that his attention had been distracted, leapt forward, and with a quick twist, wrenched the pistol from his grasp.

The Sin-Eater turned with a snarl, crouched as though he was about to spring, and then, with another swift turn, made a dash for the door.

' 'Ere!' cried the policeman, planting himself in the way. 'None o' that! You stay — ' He ended the sentence in a gasp, as a heavy blow landed in the pit of his stomach and sent him reeling backwards. Before he could recover, the fleeing man had raced along the passage and reached the door.

'Go after him!' cried Mr. Budd. 'Don't let 'im get away!'

Leek went, but he reached the door just in time to have it slammed in his face, and when he finally got it open and ran out into the street, all he could see was the red tail-light of a car disappearing round the corner. Rather dejectedly he went back into the house, to find the enraged constable asserting his authority.

'What's the game?' he demanded,

between painful gasps. 'You'd no right in 'ere, any of yer! This 'ouse's empty.'

'It's all right,' broke in Mr. Budd soothingly. 'I'm a police officer. 'Ere's me warrant card.'

He took it out of his wallet and showed it to the angry and suspicious policeman. The man's face changed as he read it.

'I'm sorry, sir,' he said apologetically, 'but 'ow was I ter know? I see the front door partly open, an' knowin' the house to be uninhabited, it was me duty to investigate.'

'You was quite right,' grunted Mr. Budd, cutting short his explanation. 'In fact, you arrived at a very opportune moment. It's a pity that feller got away, though.'

'Who was 'e, sir?' asked the policeman curiously.

'A Sin-Eater!' answered the big man, and the constable's eyes widened in astonishment. ' 'E came 'ere after a glass dragonfly. You'd better not put that in yer report, or they'll think you've been drinkin'.' He thrust the red ebony box into one of the capacious pockets of his heavy overcoat, and took a quick look round. 'We may as well be goin',' he said. 'You'd better come along with us, miss.'

The girl looked startled.

'You don't mean — ' she began, and the stout superintendent chuckled.

'No,' he said, 'I ain't detainin' yer. I meant we'd better all leave tergether. Have you got a hat, an' coat, or anythin'?'

She fetched a macintosh and an oilskin hat from somewhere in the rear of the building, and quickly put them on. Leaving the still amazed policeman to lock up the premises, Mr. Budd walked to the top of the road with Leek and the girl.

'We can drop yer at your flat,' he said, hailing a taxi that was providentially passing, and she thanked him.

'That's a nice gal,' remarked the sergeant, when she had said goodbye to them at the entrance to the flats where she lived, and Mr. Budd eyed him reprovingly.

'Don't you go getting' ideas now!' he admonished severely.

The lean sergeant reddened.

'I only said she was a nice gal!' he

protested. 'There ain't no 'arm in that, is there?'

'It all depends what you was thinkin',' said his superior. 'An' you should never judge by outward appearances, anyway.'

'What d'yer mean?' asked Leek.

'Her story sounded all right,' murmured Mr. Budd, 'and maybe it is all right, but we don't know yet.'

He dipped his fingers into his waistcoat pocket and took out a cigar.

'This is a queer, fantastic sort o' business,' he murmured, when it was alight. 'I don't think I've ever struck a queerer. Playin' cards, an' Sin-Eaters, an' glass dragonflies, an' young girls with silver 'air. Queer an' fantastic, that's what it is. An' we haven't come ter the end of it yet. You mark my words, it's going ter get queerer an' more fantastic, before very long.'

He closed his eyes, and relapsed into a silence which he did not break until the taxi drew up at the entrance to Scotland Yard.

'I don't know what yer wanted to come back 'ere for,' complained Leek, as they mounted the stairs. 'It's gettin' late an' there's nothin' more we can do ternight.'

'There's a lot I can do,' snapped the big man, opening the door of his office and switching on the light. 'I'm goin' ter be very busy just direc'ly.'

For a man who had just made such a statement his subsequent actions were certainly peculiar. Taking off his overcoat, he crossed to his desk, laid the red ebony box on the blotting pad, sat down in his chair, and, hoisting his feet up, clasped his hands loosely over his large stomach and apparently went to sleep.

The melancholy sergeant, who was used to these signs of furious activity, made himself as comfortable as possible, produced an evening newspaper and waited patiently.

For nearly an hour the big man remained motionless, and then with a sigh and a yawn, he opened his eyes and stretched himself.

'There's nothin' like a bit o' concentration when yer up against a ticklish problem,' he remarked, pulling the red ebony box towards him.

The stout superintendent opened the box and peered with a frown at the glass dragonfly. The thing must mean something, but what? He wrinkled his nose and gently scratched the extreme tip. It had no significance, so far as he could see, and yet somebody had been most anxious that it should come into his possession.

Mr. Budd lifted out the fragile ornament, and carefully examined the box. But there was nothing there. The black velvet lining was loose, and removable, and offered no place of concealment for any object, however small. Neither was there anything in the nature of a false bottom or a false lid to the box itself. If there was a secret, it must lie in the dragonfly.

The fat man searched in a drawer of his desk, and found a watchmaker's lens, which he screwed into his eye. With this adjunct, he subjected the dainty thing to an exhaustive scrutiny. At first he could find nothing that was in the least abnormal about it, and then he noticed a microscopic detail in the construction that suggested an idea.

Removing the lens from his eye, he replaced the dragonfly in the red ebony box and rose ponderously to his feet.

'Are you goin' home?' asked the weary Leek hopefully, as his superior crossed to the door.

'No,' answered Mr. Budd curtly. 'I'm going up to the Information Room. I'll be back in a minute.'

His idea of a minute was evidently rather elastic, for it was fully fifteen before he returned.

'We'll go home now,' he announced cheerfully, taking down his coat from the peg behind the door. 'We're goin' ter have a busy day termorrow.'

'What are we goin' ter do?' asked the lean sergeant, struggling into his own coat.

'We're going for a breath o' the briny,' said Mr. Budd, depositing the red ebony box in a drawer of his desk and locking it. He refused to say anything more, but hummed 'Rule, Britannia' under his breath all the way down the stairs.

Leaving the unsatisfied Leek to make

his way to his lodgings in Kennington, the stout superintendent boarded an all-night tram on the Embankment and dozed for the greater part of the journey to Streatham.

It was a quarter to two when he reached the quiet street in which he lived, and the rain had ceased. The night was very dark and damp, however, and it was with a feeling of satisfaction that he opened the neat little gate of his neat little house and started to walk up the path to his front door.

Two steps he took, and then, without warning, something dropped over his head and was drawn tightly round his neck. Before he could attempt to struggle, his arms were gripped and a hard object bored into his back.

'Keep still!' whispered a voice harshly, and half suffocated by the thick folds of the cloth over his head, Mr. Budd 'kept still'.

Hands ran swiftly over him, and he heard a muffled oath of disappointment. His arms were suddenly released, the gate slammed to, and there came the sound of retreating footsteps. The whine of an engine reached his ears, and a closed car sped past the gate as he tore the cloth from his head.

Hot and breathless, he let himself into his house and gratefully drank the beer which his Scots housekeeper had thoughtfully left for him in the dining room.

There was no great mystery concerning the reason for the attack. His assailants had been after the red ebony box, and the secret that the glass dragonfly held.

# 4

## The Shadow of the Sphinx

The morning was fine and sunny, and Mr. Budd drove to the Yard in the ancient and dingy car which was one of his most treasured possessions. It was a vintage Ford two-seater, and that it was still capable of going at all was a matter of supreme wonder to all who saw it. But go it did, and in an emergency had been known to attain the most astonishing speeds.

Leaving this dilapidated machine in the courtyard he nodded to the man on the door and went up the stairs to his office. Leek had not arrived yet, but he was informed that a man was waiting to see him.

The big man glanced at the 'blank', which the uniformed messenger placed on his desk. The space for the visitor's name was occupied by 'Oliver Frayne', and under 'Business' had been scrawled: 'Urgent — re Miss Jill Hope.'

'Where's this feller?' asked Mr. Budd. 'In the waitin' room?'

'Yes, sir,' said the messenger. 'He's been waiting some time.'

'That's what the place is for,' grunted the fat detective. 'I'll go down.'

When he entered the big, cheerless room a good-looking young man, who was impatiently staring at the portrait of a dead-and-gone Commissioner, swung round.

'You want to see me, sir?' inquired Mr. Budd.

'Are you the chap who was with Miss Hope last night?' asked the visitor, eyeing him anxiously. 'Superintendent Budd?'

The fat man nodded.

'Well, look here,' said the other, 'she's disappeared!'

'Disappeared?' echoed Mr. Budd. 'When?'

'Sometime during the night,' answered Frayne. 'I knew there'd be trouble over that job she took on, directly I heard about it. It's this man and his confounded red ebony box that's at the bottom of it — '

'Just a minute, sir,' interrupted the stout superintendent, holding up a podgy hand. 'Let's start at the beginnin' an' get thin's clear. What d'you know about this man an' the box?'

'Nothing!' declared Frayne. 'Except what Jill told me.'

He repeated, almost word for word, what the girl had said on the previous night. 'I called in to see her when she got back,' he continued. 'I only live round the corner, and I was worried about the whole business. She told me what had happened, and mentioned your name — that's why I came round here at once.'

'I'm very glad you did, sir,' said Mr. Budd seriously. 'But how do yer know the young lady's disappeared?'

'I'll tell you, if you don't keep on interrupting me,' said Frayne impatiently. 'I arranged to call for her this morning — we were going to do a round of the agents together, and look for work — but I couldn't get any answer when I reached her flat. While I was waiting, the woman who does her cleaning arrived. She's got a key, and we went in together. There was no sign of Jill, and her bed hadn't been slept in. Her handbag, with all her money, was still in the sitting room, and the lights were on. Heaven knows what's happened to her, but she never left her flat of her own accord — that's certain.'

In spite of his obvious intention to remain calm, his voice cracked a little on the last few words.

'We'll go round ter Miss Hope's flat at once, sir,' said the big man. 'Just wait 'ere a minute, will yer?'

He hurried back to his office, left a message for Leek, and rejoined Frayne. A police car took them to Russell Square, and a few minutes later they were standing in the tiny hall of the missing girl's flat. Mr. Budd cut short the voluble lamentations of the tearful charwoman, and began by making a thorough inspection of the premises.

It was a very small flat, consisting of a sitting room, a bedroom, a microscopic bathroom, and a little kitchen. A window in the kitchen was open, and an examination of the catch showed that it had been forced. An iron stairway, which communicated with all the flats, passed near this window, and down into a small courtyard, to which easy access from the street could be gained through a low iron gate.

'The burglar's delight!' murmured Mr. Budd when he saw this. 'This is the way they came, without any doubt.'

He found nothing else that was at all helpful, and after assuring the worried and anxious Frayne that he would do his best to find the girl, he left. Calling in to the local police station before he went back to the Yard, he reported the matter to the inspector in charge, and arranged for a man to be sent round to Greville Mansions to take charge of the flat.

His first action, when he got back to the Yard, was to set in motion the usual routine inquiry, which is followed in the case of a disappearance such as Jill Hope's, and satisfied that he could do nothing more for the moment, made his way to his office.

Leek had arrived, and was perched on his usual chair reading the morning newspaper. He looked up as the big man came in.

'I thought you was gettin' here early?'

he grumbled. 'If I'd known, I wouldn't 'ave hurried over me breakfast.'

'I've been 'ere for hours!' snapped Mr. Budd, going over to his desk and taking the red ebony box out of the drawer. 'Breakfast! You mean yer lunch, don't yer?'

The lean sergeant did not pursue the subject.

'What about this trip ter the sea?' he began.

'We're going now,' broke in his superior. 'Have yer got yer bucket an' spade?'

'Where are we goin'?' asked Leek, disdaining any reply to this frivolous question.

'Clacton,' answered Mr. Budd briefly. 'Come on!'

He did not offer any explanation for the expedition, and the curious sergeant was forced to possess his puzzled soul in patience.

At Colchester they stopped for petrol and a hasty meal, starting on the remaining eighteen-mile run to Clacton just before half-past two. The ancient car sped along gallantly, if rather noisily, and they reached their destination in under three-quarters of an hour. Mr. Budd drove slowly along the front, in the direction of Frinton, and presently stopped at a filling station.

'We'll have ter leave the car 'ere,' he said. 'Much as I dislike walkin', we'll have ter go the rest of the way on foot.'

'Where are we makin' for?' asked the sergeant, but Mr. Budd was already arranging with one of the garage attendants to look after the car, and if he heard the question, he ignored it.

It was a beautiful afternoon. The sun shone in an almost cloudless sky, and there was just sufficient wind to ripple the surface of the sea. Mr. Budd ambled gently along the remainder of the front, with his hat pushed to the back of his head, his hands thrust deep into his pockets, and his sleepy-looking eyes half closed.

In a little while the front ended, and they found themselves alone on the steep white cliffs. Fifty feet below, the sea was foaming gently across a wide stretch of sand, and away in the distance the pier showed faintly.

They had reached a desolate spot, remote from both Clacton and the adjoining town of Frinton, when the big man stopped suddenly.

'Can you 'ear anythin'?' he asked softly.

Leek listened. He could hear the roar of the surf and the swish of the shingle, and the sad cries of the wheeling gulls. And then, just as he was on the act of shaking his head, he heard another sound.

It was like the ghost of music; an elusive, sighing, indescribably mournful sound which seemed to creep in whispering harmony along the ground and weave gossamer melody in the clouds.

'What is it?' he muttered in astonishment.

'Let's see if we can find out,' answered Mr. Budd below his breath.

They moved forward, the ghost-music filling the air around them with its plaintive cadence, and presently came in sight of a bungalow, set dangerously near to the edge of the cliff.

It was a large building, of peculiar design, ornamented with grotesque turrets, and it was closely shuttered. No smoke rose from the queer chimneys, and no signs of life were to be seen. And yet the whole place was vibrating with that strange unearthly music. The effect was so weird that Leek felt a little shiver pass uncomfortably down his spine.

'Look there!' murmured Mr. Budd suddenly, and pointed.

The sergeant looked in the direction of his stubby finger, and saw that the sun, striking the house squarely, sent a shadow sprawling in dense black along the cliff top — and the shadow formed a perfect silhouette of the Sphinx.

# 5

## The Seven Sleepers

'Do you remember the words on them playin' cards that was sent to poor Pettegew?' said Mr. Budd in a low voice, staring at the sprawling black shadow. ''By the shadow of the Sphinx an aeolian harp murmurs'.'

'What makes it like that?' asked the wondering Leek.

'The shadow?' Mr. Budd looked at the bungalow and pursed his thick lips. 'All them turrets an' what-nots, I should think. It seems ter me as if they was put there for that partic'ler purpose. Let's see if there's anyone at 'ome.'

He walked towards the place, with the sergeant at his heels. A square of weed-grown and neglected garden was enclosed by a white-painted fence, in which had been set a gate that was secured with a stout chain and padlock.

The fat detective surveyed the exterior of the building, but there was no sign of life to be seen, and the only sound that reached their ears was the eerie strains of the music. After a pause, he laboriously climbed the gate, followed by Leek, and walked ponderously up to the front porch.

It seemed a futile proceeding to ring the bell, but he did so as a matter of precaution, and was inwardly surprised when his action was instantly productive of results. There was the sound of a chair being scraped back from a table, and footsteps shuffled towards the door.

Chain, lock, and latch were unfastened in turn, and the door opened to reveal a bent old man with dirty white hair, who peered out at them malevolently.

'Whatcher want?' he growled ungraciously, displaying a mouthful of broken yellow teeth.

'We was attracted by the queer music,' said Mr. Budd pleasantly. 'It comes from 'ere, don't it?'

'It do,' answered the old man sullenly. 'It's a kind of an 'arp fixed in the winder at the back. When I opens the winder, it plays like wot yer 'ear now.'

He spoke as if he were being civil under compulsion, and it struck the big man that he had been instructed to greet any curious inquirers more or less respectfully.

'Could we 'ave a look at this thing — an aeolian harp, I believe they call it?' he said.

'You can come through, if yer like,' said the old man, after a momentary hesitation. 'The place is shut up, an' I'm the caretaker. Lonely sort a job it is, too, an' no error.'

'It doesn't strike me as bein' exactly lively,' agreed Mr. Budd, as the other led the way across a square hall and through a large room that was full of furniture in holland wrappers.

'Lively!' The old man gave a cracked laugh. 'I reckon the North Pole 'ud be more lively!' He pulled back a curtain from an archway and they found themselves in a kitchen that was filled with the music of the harp. 'There yer are,' said the caretaker, and jerked his head at the window.

It was a large one, extending from floor to ceiling, and the catgut strings had been stretched across the lower half. As the wind blew gently through them, they gave forth their plaintive music.

Mr. Budd examined the arrangement cursorily, and then calmly seated himself in a chair by the table.

'You can close the window — now,' he said slowly.

The caretaker gave him a startled glance.

'Whatcher mean?' he demanded doubtfully.

'I'm the man you've been waitin' for,' said the stout superintendent. He was taking a chance, and he knew it. He was acting entirely on a supposition that might quite easily be wrong.

'I don't know what yer talkin' about,' growled the old man, and for answer Mr. Budd took the red ebony box from his overcoat pocket, opened it, and exhibited the glass dragonfly.

The caretaker stared at it, and then scrutinised the big man with a new respect in his manner.

'It's nigh on three weeks I've bin waitin' fer yer, sir,' he breathed. 'Some'ow I got an idea yer'd come at night. Am I to do everythin' as was arranged?'

Mr. Budd nodded, and there was relief in his heart. His wits had not led him astray.

'Then I'll be getting' off, sir,' said the old man surprisingly. 'Lummy, but I'll be glad ter get a sight o' Lon'un again arter this 'ole! The sea's all very well fer them wot likes it, but give me the Borough on a Saturd'y night.' He wagged his head and winked. 'Blue butterflies, sir!'

'Eh?' said the astonished Mr. Budd.

'That's wot I was ter tell yer,' said the caretaker.

'Oh, yes, of course!' grunted the big man, without the slightest idea what he was talking about. 'Blue butterflies?'

'That's right, sir,' said the old man. 'I'll be gettin' along now.'

He hurried away, and Mr. Budd was contemplating the advisability of detaining him, when he had an inspiration. It was probable that the old man would call on the person who had employed him, to make a report. Anyway, it was a chance not to be missed.

'Foller this feller when he leaves,' he whispered to Leek, and the lean sergeant nodded. 'Don't let 'im out of yer sight, and try an' find out who he sees.'

In two or three minutes the old man returned, equipped for his journey in a threadbare overcoat and a battered hat. His luggage consisted of a dingy leather bag, held shut by a piece of rope.

'I'm off now, sir,' he said. 'You'll find them in the big bedroom.'

He nodded, winked again, and then went shuffling off through the curtained archway. A second later the front door slammed.

'Off you go, too!' snapped Mr. Budd, and Leek obeyed. Left to himself, the stout superintendent took a cigar from his pocket and lit it. Then he went over to the window and closed it, cutting off the strains of music as though he had turned a switch on a radio set. What had the old man meant by 'them'? They, whatever or who-ever they were, were in the big bedroom.

With the cigar between his teeth, Mr. Budd began an exploration of the bungalow. There was nothing in the living room but dust and old furniture, and he turned his attention to the sleeping quarters. Three of the rooms that he looked into were quite small, and of these two were empty. The third contained a bed and a few articles of furniture, and had evidently been used by the old caretaker. Coming to the fourth door, he heard a sound and stopped to listen. It was the sound of regular and heavy breathing!

His hand closed over the butt of the automatic with which he had thoughtfully provided himself, and, creeping to the door, he twisted the handle and threw it wide.

The room was a large one, dimly lit by the faint rays of the sunlight that filtered in through the chinks in the wooden shutters that covered the window, and it was devoid of furniture with the exception of seven mattresses that were ranged round the walls. And on these mattresses lay seven men apparently fast asleep!

'The seven sleepers,' murmured Mr. Budd in utter amazement. ' 'By the shadow of the Sphinx an aeolian harp murmurs to the seven sleepers'! It's crazy, but it's first-class prophecy!'

He entered the room and took a closer view of the sleepers. They were all well-dressed, but of widely divergent types and ages. He watched them through half-closed eyes for a few seconds, rubbing his chin in perplexity, and then, passing from one to the other, he examined each with care, finally subjecting them all to a hearty shaking. But none of them woke.

'Drugged, I s'pose,' he muttered dubiously when he had done his best to rouse the sleepers, without success. 'Though it must be a queer kind o' drug.'

He searched all their pockets, but they were empty. There was nothing to show who the men were, or how they had come to fall into that cataleptic state.

Thoroughly and completely bewildered, he left the sleeping men and went back to the kitchen. The thing to do, of course, was to get a doctor to them as soon as

161

possible; but that would mean leaving the bungalow. The men, however, certainly ought to have immediate attention and, if they could be brought round, might offer some valuable information.

After a great deal of thought, Mr. Budd decided to risk leaving the place untenanted and go in search of a doctor. He found a key to the room in which the seven sleepers lay, and carefully locked the door. He also locked the main door, and then set off for the garage where he had left his car.

The journey into Clacton did not take him long, and he called first at the police station, where he interviewed the inspector.

That worthy man listened in astonishment to what he had to say. He knew of the bungalow, but had no idea to whom it belonged. It had, he said, been built a year or eighteen months previously.

'I'll ring up the divisional surgeon, sir,' he said. 'He only lives in the next street, an' I expect he'll be at home now.'

The divisional surgeon was at home, and came hurrying round immediately.

He was a pleasant-faced, capable-looking man, immensely interested in what the fat detective had to tell him.

'It sounds remarkable,' he said. 'I'll come along with you right away.'

He had his own car, and he followed in it while Mr. Budd led the way with a stolid constable seated beside him. They drove to within a hundred yards of the bungalow since this time the big man knew exactly what he was looking for, and where it was located. Before, he had merely followed the direction contained in the wings of the glass dragonfly. It had occurred to him that the delicate green threads that formed the markings might be shorthand symbols, and a visit to one of the experts in the Information Room had confirmed his theory. The message said simply: 'Between Clacton and Frinton'; and to that spot he had come without the slightest idea of what he was likely to find.

Everything in the bungalow was as he had left it. The seven men still lay asleep, and with the constable and Mr. Budd looking on, the doctor made his examination. He completed it in silence, and when he had finished he rose to his feet with a face of blank surprise.

'This is the most extraordinary thing!' he exclaimed. 'The most extraordinary thing!'

'Maybe I'll agree with yer when I know what you're talkin' about,' grunted Mr. Budd. 'What's the matter with these fellers?'

'Trypanosoma Gambiense,' answered the doctor. 'Every one of these men is suffering from an advanced stage of West African sleeping-sickness!'

# 6

## The Message on the Playing Card

Mr. Budd heard the doctor's diagnosis outwardly unmoved.

'H'm,' he remarked, stroking one of his flabby cheeks gently, 'that's rather an unusual complaint, ain't it?'

'Most unusual!' declared the doctor. 'In fact, it is practically unknown in this country. The disease is caused by a parasite called Trypanosoma. These men have been down with the sickness for a considerable time.'

'How long will it take 'em to recover?' asked the big man.

The doctor pursed his lips, and shook his head gravely.

'That is quite impossible to tell,' he replied. 'It is more than likely that they will never recover. The majority of the cases of sleeping-sickness have proved fatal. These men should receive a specialist's treatment at once.'

Mr. Budd transferred the stroking process from his cheek to his large nose, and frowned.

'I don't want a lot o' publicity about this,' he said. 'Wouldn't it be possible ter treat 'em here?'

'No,' answered the doctor without hesitation. 'They must be removed to a hospital. This disease is very rare, and very little is known about it. It is absolutely necessary that an attempted cure should be carried out under the most advantageous circumstances.'

The stout superintendent's frown deepened. It was impossible to go against the advice of the doctor, but he had no wish that the discovery of the sleeping men should become public property. It might warn the people who were behind this strange business and spoil whatever chance there was of catching them.

'Well,' he said at last reluctantly, 'I s'pose, if you say so, it'll have ter be done. But I want it kept as quiet as possible, in the interests of justice. I'll rely on you fer that.'

The divisional surgeon promised to do his best. He undertook to get in immediate touch with a specialist and arrange for the removal of the seven sleepers, under cover of darkness. With this the big man had to be content.

'What do you suppose is behind all this?' said the doctor, as he walked with Mr. Budd through the gathering dusk to the place where they had left the cars.

The fat man shook his head wearily.

'I haven't the least idea,' he declared candidly. 'I'm just pickin' up stray bits 'ere an' there, but what they all mean is more'n I can tell yer.'

'It's amazing!' muttered the doctor. 'Those men must have been inoculated with the disease in some way. It's impossible that they could have contracted it otherwise.'

'Well, it's a new one on me,' said Mr. Budd. 'Comes from West Africa, yer say? H'm!'

He had suddenly remembered that Mr. Pettegew had, according to the house agent, also come from Africa.

It was almost dark when Mr. Budd

reached Clacton and once more paid a visit to the police station.

'I've left your man on guard at the bungalow,' he said to the inspector, 'an' I want yer to send two more along ter keep him company. The place is ter be watched day an' night, an' anyone who comes near it is ter be detained. I shall be comin' down again termorrow. Is that clear?'

The local inspector declared that it was quite clear, and Mr. Budd took his leave and started back to London.

He arrived at the Yard, tired and hungry, and, as he was going in, almost collided with Oliver Frayne.

'I was just coming to see you,' panted the young man. 'I've had a message — '

'Come inside!' said the big man wearily. 'You can't tell me out 'ere.'

He led the agitated Oliver into a small room opening off the vestibule. Frayne pulled an envelope from his pocket.

'This came by the last post tonight,' he said. 'What can we do? We must do something at once — '

'Let me see what yer've got first,' interrupted Mr. Budd, and took the envelope from the other's hand. It was addressed to 'Oliver Frayne, Esquire, 29A, Gower Street, W.C.1,' and contained a single playing card — the ace of hearts. Across the face of this had been scrawled in pencil a terse message:

'Get the red ebony box if you want to save the girl's life says the Sin-Eater. Pin this to the door as a signal.'

'You've got the box, haven't you?' asked Frayne anxiously. 'You must give it me — '

'Now, just a minute, sir,' murmured Mr. Budd, twisting the card about in his podgy fingers. 'This wants thinkin' about — '

'We've no time to think about it!' cried the young man impatiently. 'Don't you see what it says? If we don't do what they ask, Jill will — '

'The young lady's safe enough fer a bit,' broke in the big man. 'No 'arm 'ull come to 'er until they see what's goin' to happen. She's the other half of the bargain.' He fingered the fleshy folds of his chin and closed his eyes, while Frayne waited in an agony of impatience and apprehension. 'I think it 'ud be a good idea if you did what they ask,' he said after an interval of thought. 'Yes, I think it 'ud be a very good idea. They want the box, an' they shall 'ave it.'

Frayne's strained look relaxed a little.

'Give it to me,' he said quickly, 'and I'll go straight back — '

'Now, don't you be in such a 'urry!' muttered the fat detective. 'I know 'ow yer feelin', but there's no need to rush things. Just let me work this out, will yer?'

He pulled forward a chair, sat down, and, leaning back, let his chin droop on to his chest. He remained in this position for so long without sound or movement that the distracted Oliver thought he had fallen asleep, and was on the point of taking drastic steps to wake him, when he suddenly opened his eyes and sat up.

'Here you are,' he said, taking the red ebony box out of his overcoat pocket. 'An' here's the playin' card. Go 'ome an' pin that card on the door at twelve o'clock. Maybe somebody'll call. If they do, give 'em the box, but don't say nothin', an' don't put that card out before twelve.'

'What are you going to do?' asked Frayne, taking the box and the card and slipping them into his pocket.

'I'm goin' ter wait an' see what happens,' answered the big man, yawning. 'Now, off yer go, an' don't worry. No 'arm'll come to your young lady.'

He escorted Oliver off the premises and went up to his office. Lifting the house telephone, he called an extension number.

'I want three men sent ter Gower Street at once,' he said. 'They're to watch No. 29A an' foller anybody who calls after twelve o'clock tonight. I don't want 'em interfered with; I just want 'em follered, understand?'

Apparently the person he had been speaking to did understand, for he put the telephone back on its rest with a sigh of relief. Sitting down at his desk, he pressed a bell, and when a messenger came in answer to the ring he sent him for coffee and sandwiches.

While he waited for the refreshment to

be brought he began to sort over his ideas. The message received by Oliver Frayne proved that the girl was in the hands of the Sin-Eater, and not the unknown man who had sent her to the empty house in Great Oram Street. He had already been in possession of the red ebony box. It was the man who called himself the Sin-Eater who was anxious to get hold of it — so anxious, indeed, that he had gone to the risk of abducting the girl for no other purpose. His reason was pretty clear. He wanted to know where the bungalow was situated, and was relying on the glass dragonfly to supply him with the information. But what was the attraction of the bungalow? Why was the place of such importance that its whereabouts had to be revealed in this roundabout fashion? Did the secret lie in the seven sleeping men, or in that cryptic phrase of the old caretaker's — 'Blue Butterflies'?

Mr. Budd frowned and scratched the lobe of his right ear.

The stout superintendent swallowed his coffee and poured out a second cup. The whole business was very involved.

Someone was working to convey information to the Sin-Eater, in a form that only he would understand, while an unknown third person was apparently trying to put a spoke in the wheel. That seemed as far as it was possible to get, at the moment. The cause, or causes, which had set in motion the fantastic series of effects remained obscure.

He had finished the last of his sandwiches and settled back in his chair to enjoy one of his evil-smelling cigars, when Leek came in.

The lean sergeant was looking more miserable and lugubrious than ever, and dropped into his chair with a weary sigh.

'Well,' said Mr. Budd, 'what happened?'

'Nothin',' answered Leek, shaking his head mournfully. 'I might've saved meself the trouble o' followin' that feller. He didn't try ter see no one. All 'e did was ter get tight!'

'An' then?' prompted the big man.

'There ain't no 'then',' said the sergeant gloomily. 'That's jest all that 'appened! I tailed 'im from the station to a pub at the

Elephant an' Castle, an' there 'e stuck all the blessed evenin'. He'd 'ave stuck there all night, only they threw 'im out, an' then he was pinched for bein' drunk an' disorderly.'

'Well, that's somethin', anyway! grunted Mr. Budd. 'We know where 'e's ter be found.'

'We know 'is name, too,' said the sergeant. 'I 'ad a word with the feller who pinched 'im, after they'd locked him up, and 'e told me 'is name was Hutchin, an' he was pretty well-known in the district. He's 'ad several convictions, an' seems ter be a thorough bad lot.'

'That doesn't surprise me,' said the stout superintendent, taking his cigar from his mouth and examining the end thoughtfully. 'H'm, I'll have a word with Mr. Hutchin termorrer. Maybe he's goin' ter get another conviction, an' the sentence 'ull be a bigger one than 'e's ever had before.'

The telephone-bell rang as he finished speaking, and he stretched out his arm for the receiver.

'Hello!' he called into the mouthpiece,

and a voice answered instantly.

'This is Detective-Constable Matson speaking, sir,' it said rapidly. 'A man called five minutes ago at 29A, Gower Street, and rang the bell. The door was opened by another man, who handed the first a parcel. The first man then walked quickly away, and was followed by the other man — '

Mr. Budd uttered an exclamation of annoyance.

'What did he want ter do that for?' he muttered crossly.

'I beg your pardon, sir?' said the puzzled man at the other end of the wire.

'It's all right, Matson,' growled Mr. Budd. 'Go on.'

'They both went in the direction of Southampton Row,' continued the detective. 'Wilson an' Lane are tailin' 'em. What d'you want me to do?'

'Nothin',' replied the fat man. 'You can come back here.'

He hung up the receiver and glowered at his desk. So Oliver Frayne had decided to take an active part in the game, had he? he thought, and shook his head dubiously. He was afraid that it might be a case of too many cooks spoiling the broth he had so carefully prepared.

# 7

## The Factory in Mickle Street

Oliver Frayne returned to Gower Street with his mind full of misgivings. He let himself in with his key, and, going up to his room, paced up and down in a frenzy of uncertainty, smoking jerkily at a cigarette.

It was pretty certain that the police would take steps to have the house watched and follow whoever called for the box; but supposing they missed him? It was more than likely that the Sin-Eater would expect some such move, and allow for it, and then they would be no nearer finding Jill than they had been before. And the finding of Jill was all that Oliver cared about.

He came to his decision just before the clock on his mantelshelf warned him that it was nearing twelve. He would follow the man who came for the box himself, and then, if he succeeded in giving the police the slip, there would still be a chance of finding out where they had taken the girl.

The possibility of taking an active part in the proceedings soothed him, and, creeping downstairs, he pinned the playing card to the front door and waited.

The shrill peal of the bell came almost immediately, so quickly that Oliver concluded that the ringer must have been watching for the signal. His hand closed round the red ebony box in his pocket, and he opened the door.

A man stood on the step, his face scarcely visible between the turned-down brim of his hat and the upturned collar of his coat.

'I've called for the box,' he said huskily.

Oliver put it into his hand, without a word, and the man turned quickly and walked away. Waiting for a moment to give him time to get a little way ahead, Oliver slipped out and closed the door softly behind him. He could see the other walking rapidly up the street, and as he went in pursuit he looked hastily round to see if he could catch a glimpse of the detective, whom he felt sure must be some-where in the vicinity. But there was no sign of him, and he never gave the taxi which was crawling along in his wake a second glance. Taxis were fairly common in the district, and there was nothing to show that this particular cab was driven by Detective-Constable Wilson of the C.I.D.

The man in front turned the corner into Southampton Row, and set briskly off in the direction of Kingsway. At the corner of Theobalds Road he stopped, gave a sharp look round, and boarded a tramcar that was just descending into the tunnel. Oliver saw him mount the steps to the upper deck, and, running forward, caught the tram himself.

When it emerged on to the Embank-ment, the man alighted and waited under the arch of the bridge. Presently another tram came along, and he swung himself on to the platform, once again mounting to the top. Oliver took his place inside, near the door, and bought a ticket for the full length of the run, since he had no idea how far the man was going.

It was not very far, as it proved, for at

Vauxhall he got off, crossed the wide thoroughfare by the station, and plunged into the gloom of a side street, with Oliver at his heels. Up one street and down another they went, until Oliver had completely lost all sense of his where-abouts in this unfamiliar neighbourhood.

At last the man turned into a narrow, ill-lighted cul-de-sac, which, according to the sign on the corner that Oliver just managed to glimpse in the stray rays from a street standard, bore the name of Mickle Street.

It was an undesirable-looking place, lined on either side with high buildings, black and smoke-grimed, which appeared to consist for the most part of warehouses.

Before the wide, wooden gates of one of these the man stopped, pushed open a wicket and disappeared within. Oliver waited for a second or two farther down the street, and then cautiously approached and inspected the place.

From the look of it, it had at one time been a soap factory. The dirty, soot-encrusted walls still bore dingy advertisements painted on them, recommending various kinds of soap, and the gaunt framework of a crane projected like a gallows from an upper floor. That it was now empty was evident by the tattered auctioneers' bills, which had been pasted on most of the windows.

Oliver tried the wicket through which the man had vanished, and rather to his surprise it opened. Beyond was a square yard, full of rubbish and old boxes, and after a moment's hesitation he stepped inside.

It was very dark and he could see very little, but after a while he managed to make out the vague oblong of an open door that formed a patch of blackness in the side of the dilapidated old building.

Picking his way through the litter in the yard, he went over to this and listened.

He could hear a faint sound from somewhere within that sounded like the rumble of voices, but even as he listened it ceased. This seemed the way the man must have gone, however, and he slipped quietly inside.

He found himself in a vast space, bounded by whitewashed walls and dimly lighted by a faint glow which percolated

through the dirty windows from the street
without. The wooden floor was strewn
with old paper and rotting straw, and
there was an aromatic odour that made
his nostrils tingle. The place, which appeared
to cover the whole of the ground floor of
the empty factory, was deserted, but in
one corner was a staircase that led upward,
and towards this he crept.

Exercising the greatest caution to avoid
making any noise that would give his
presence away, Oliver mounted the wooden
stairs, emerging presently through a square
hole into a bare chamber that was almost
a replica of the lower floor. The only difference was that a partition had been built
across one end, dividing it from the rest,
in which had been set a door. And from
beneath this door a dim light trickled.

Almost holding his breath, he tiptoed
across the intervening expanse of rubbish-
strewn floor and, reaching the door, bent
down and looked through the keyhole.

At first he could see very little, for the
light was dim; but presently he was able
to distinguish something of the room and
its occupants.

It was devoid of furniture except for a rickety table on which a candle burned stuck in a pool of congealed grease. On one side of this stood the man whom he had followed from Gower Street, and on the other, bending over the red ebony box, was a second man, whose face was partially covered by a handkerchief that reached from his eyes to his chin.

Oliver thought that these two men were the only occupants of the room until he shifted his position slightly and obtained a fresh viewpoint.

And then he saw Jill Hope.

She was half-sitting, half-lying, in one corner, her silver hair gleaming in the yellow light from the candle. About her mouth was a gag, and her hands and ankles had been tied with thin cord. She was staring with wide, fear-darkened eyes at the man who was intently examining the contents of the red ebony box, and Oliver's relief at finding her was swallowed up in a sudden fury against the man who had been responsible for bringing her to this place.

Moving to see better, disaster overtook

him. His foot slipped on some greasy substance on the floor and he overbalanced, falling heavily against the door. It flew open under his weight and he went sprawling ungracefully into the room!

His sudden appearance created a sensation. The girl uttered a strangled gasp, and the man who had come to Gower Street sprang back with a squeal of alarm. Only the man who had been peering into the red ebony box remained outwardly unmoved. His hand dipped into the pocket of his coat with the speed of light and emerged holding an automatic pistol.

'You'd better stay where you are!' he snapped harshly, as Oliver started to scramble to his feet. 'Stay where you are — and keep still!'

'It's the feller who give me the box!' muttered the other man, and the Sin-Eater's hard eyes above the handkerchief narrowed.

'Oh, is that who it is?' he whispered softly. 'Mr. Oliver Frayne, eh? What are you doing here, Mr. Frayne?'

'I followed him,' said Oliver angrily,

jerking his head towards the other man. 'What have you done to Miss Hope, you brute — '

'She is unharmed,' interrupted the Sin-Eater calmly, 'and there is no reason why she shouldn't remain so. I have no further interest in her, now that I have got what I wanted. We are going now, and you can release Miss Hope at your leisure. I'm afraid I shall have to lock you in, but that is a precaution which you will understand.'

He moved over to the door, took a key from his pocket with his free hand, and fitted it in the lock.

'Bring the candle,' he said to his companion, and when the man had joined him: 'It may take you some time to break your way out, Mr. Frayne, but I've no doubt you'll manage it eventually. Perhaps you will have the police to help you. I should scarcely think you were the only one who followed my messenger.'

He signed to the man with the candle to precede him, went out quickly and slammed the door. Oliver heard the key turn in the lock, and the sound of their retreating footsteps, as he got to his feet and struck a match. His first thought was for the girl, and, going over to where she lay, he bent down.

'Are you all right, dear?' he asked anxiously, and she nodded. The match lasted just long enough for him to locate the knot, which held the gag in place and then went out. It was not easy to untie the knot in the dark, but he had no means of cutting it, and he had just succeeded in loosening it when there came a faint cry from somewhere below, and a dull, thudding noise. It sounded as if one of the men had fallen down the stairway, and Oliver gave a little grunt of satisfaction, with the fervent hope that he had broken his neck.

'There we are!' he said, pulling the gag away and turning his attention to the cords at her wrists. 'I'll soon have you free, Jill, and then we'll see about getting out of this beastly place.'

'I don't think I shall be able to move,' she whispered huskily. 'I'm all numb.'

'That'll soon pass,' said Oliver reassuringly. 'My stars, these cords are tight!' He broke off suddenly and sniffed. An acrid odour had reached his nostrils — the faint but unmistakable smell of burning.

'What's the matter?' asked the girl.

'Nothing,' he muttered, and redoubled his efforts to undo the cords that bound her. A horrible suspicion, born of that faint smell, had come to him, but he had no wish to alarm the girl unnecessarily. The perspiration was streaming down his face, and his fingers were sore by the time he had succeeded in untying the last knot and flung the cords away.

Jill stifled the cry that rose in her throat, and clenched her teeth, for the pain induced by the restored circulation was agonising.

'Rub your wrists and ankles, darling,' said Oliver, straightening up. 'I'm going to have a look at this door.'

He struck another match, went over and shook the handle. But both the door and the partition had been solidly built, and even when he flung his whole weight against it, it made no impression.

The smell of burning was more pronounced, and his suspicion became a certainty.

He lit a third match and turned to Jill. She lay quite still, her head drooping forward on her breast, and when he reached her he discovered that she had fainted.

With white face and knitted brows, he glanced about him. Something must be done, and done soon. There was a small window in one wall, and going over to this he wrenched back the hasp and opened it. Thrusting out his head, he peered down into the street below. Escape that way was hopeless. It was a sheer drop of nearly fifty feet.

He was in the act of turning back, when he saw something that brought a chill to his heart. Like streamers of cobwebs floating in the air, little threads of grey smoke were pouring from the cracks in the lower windows.

His suspicions had been correct. The factory was on fire!

# 8

## What Mr. Hutchin Knew

Oliver checked the sudden panic that threatened to overwhelm him as he realised the full horror of the situation. The only possible hope lay in keeping a cool head.

Leaning out of the window, he shouted until he was hoarse, but no answering voice came to warn him that his cry had been heard.

A glance below showed him that the fire was gaining ground. The feathery smoke had changed to dense black clouds, shot with red and orange tongues, and the crackling was giving place to a deep roar.

Oliver withdrew his head and wiped his damp face. Once again he tried an assault on the door, but it resisted all his efforts.

The air was growing unpleasantly hot, and the acrid tang of smoke caught him by the throat and set him coughing. He went back to the window and looked out. Sheets of flame were now lapping in and out of the ground floor windows, where the heat had shattered the glass, and the clouds of smoke blotted out the street. The whole of the lower floor was blazing furiously.

Oliver stumbled back to the girl, and struck his last remaining match. She was still unconscious, and for this he was thankful. Just before the feeble flame of the match dwindled and died he saw that the room was full of a blue haze of smoke, and that more was pouring in under the door.

The distant jangle of a bell attracted his attention, and, with a wave of hope sweeping over him, he staggered back to the window. The sound of the jangling bell drew rapidly nearer, and was followed by others from far and near. Somebody had seen the fire and circulated a brigade call. From out of the billowing smoke Oliver heard the shrill, excited chatter of voices, and tried to shout. But his throat, dry and rasped by the smoke, refused to deliver anything but a hoarse whisper, which was drowned by the roar of the fire.

And then the engines came thundering into the cul-de-sac from every quarter of London.

The narrow street became an inferno of steam and smoke, daubed scarlet by the flames. And Oliver watched with despair in his heart. Nobody would suspect that there was anyone in the doomed building, and he and Jill would be dead long before the holocaust was subdued.

In a desperate effort to attract attention he waved and shouted, but the noise of the fire and the engines drowned his hoarse cries as the blanket of swirling smoke hid him from view.

Panting and exhausted, with smarting eyes and raw throat, he leaned heavily on the narrow sill, staring hopelessly into the void below.

Out of it suddenly emerging through the dense smoke like the spire of a church above a ground fog, appeared the top of a tall escape. It loomed nearer and closer, and the red, smoke-grimed face of a startled fireman stared at him from a few feet away.

Oliver gave a husky cry of thankfulness, and the man shouted something. The escape came nearer until it was almost touching the sill of the little window.

'Come on!' cried the fireman, stretching out a helping hand. 'And look sharp! The floor you're on may go at any minute!'

'There's somebody else,' gasped Oliver, and staggered to where the girl lay. As he lifted her she moaned slightly and began to whisper incoherently. Muttering soothingly, he half-carried and half-dragged her to the window and, hoisting her over the sill, surrendered her to the arms of the fireman.

'Anybody else inside?' asked the man, and Oliver shook his head.

'Then get a move on!' said the fireman. 'I'll take the lady down, and you can follow.'

He began to descend the escape, and Oliver swung his leg over the sill. The floor collapsed behind him as he clutched at the ladder, and a sheet of flame covered the inside of the window. Help had come only just in time. Dizzy and shaking, he went down foot by foot, and the last thing he remembered was eager hands helping him to the ground. Then his knees gave way and the lurid glare of the fire changed suddenly to blackness.

★  ★  ★

'What a night!' grunted Mr. Budd wearily, just as the first glimmer of dawn was beginning to pale the eastern sky. 'Nothin' but excitement, an' very little ter show fer it.'

'I could sleep standin' on me feet,' said Leek, yawning widely.

'You mostly do!' snapped the big man, leaning back in his chair. 'You'd better go 'ome fer an hour or two. There's nothin' more you can do. But don't get 'ere later than ten o'clock; I shall want yer then.'

The melancholy sergeant departed, and the fat detective closed his eyes and settled down for a short nap.

The night had, in truth, been a busy one, and he had not long returned to the Yard from Mickle Street. Detective-Constable Lane, who had been inside the taxi driven by his colleague, Wilson, had followed Frayne and the messenger to the deserted factory, and, acting on instructions, had reported to Mr. Budd. He had been told to keep the place under observation, and had been the first to discover that it was on fire and give the alarm. He had not seen anyone leave, and it was his assertion to the captain of the fire brigade that there was somebody in the burning building that had eventually resulted in the rescue of Oliver and the girl.

When Mr. Budd had been notified of the fire he had at once driven to Mickle Street, and had been present when Jill and Oliver had been saved.

There was nothing seriously the matter with either of them, and, although a doctor was sent for, they had both recovered before he arrived.

The big man had interviewed them without much result. The girl's story was brief and contained little that he did not already know. She had been on the point of going to bed, when she had heard a noise in the kitchen, and gone along to see what it was. The kitchen had been in darkness, and before she had had time to switch on the light an arm had been flung round her neck and a pad of chloroform pressed over her face. She had remembered nothing more until she found herself, tied up and gagged, in the room where Oliver Frayne had discovered her. There she had stayed, alone and without food, until the man who called himself the Sin-Eater had come to await the arrival of the messenger.

Mr. Budd had expected to add very little to his knowledge, and he was not disappointed. The reason why the Sin-Eater should have set fire to the factory puzzled him until he heard Oliver's account of what had happened, and the sound of the cry and the fall that he had heard. Then it seemed pretty clear. The man with the candle had stumbled on the stairs, and the candle had probably fallen from his hand among the litter of paper and straw. It was only feasible to suppose that the start of the fire had been an accident for there was no other reasonable explanation.

The way by which the Sin-Eater and his companion had left, without Lane

seeing them, he had found when a fireman had shown him an entrance to the
factory yard, which opened into another
street running parallel with Mickle Street.

The messenger had been instructed to
come to the front entrance, with the
intention, obviously, of misleading anyone
who might be following him into thinking
that it was the only one.

Leaving the firemen still battling with
the blazing factory, the stout superintendent returned to the Yard, neither elated
nor depressed with his night's work.

That the Sin-Eater had got away
worried him not at all. It had never been
his intention to detain the man. By
arresting him prematurely, all hope of
discovering the real truth behind the
extraordinary business might be jeopar-
dised. And sooner or later, now that he
had got the glass dragonfly, he would go
to the bungalow on the cliff top, and from
there he wouldn't find it so easy to get
away.

Until half-past nine he occupied
himself in drafting out a list of certain
items of information that he required, and

when this had then dispatched to the department, which dealt with such things, he put on his overcoat and drove to the Borough.

Mr. Daniel Hutchin, having appeared before an unsympathetic magistrate and been fined twenty shillings, was gloomily leaving the police court, when he felt himself taken affectionately by the arm, and, turning, found the big man who had come to the bungalow beside him.

'Been 'aving a bit of a spree ter celebrate yer return, ain't yer?' murmured Mr. Budd in a voice of friendly understanding. 'Well, well, I dare say yer could do with a nice cup o' coffee, eh? There's a teashop over there that'll do nicely.'

He piloted his reluctant companion across the road, and pushed him into the small restaurant.

'I can't see 'ow you knew,' muttered the old man, when they were facing each other over a marble-topped table.

'Now, don't you go worryin' yer head about that,' said Mr. Budd soothingly. 'You'll have plenty to worry about, unless you come clean.'

Mr. Hutchin regarded him with a startled expression on his yellow face.

'Wotcher gettin' at?' he said.

The big man waited while the waitress set two cups of coffee before them, and then he answered.

'I'm gettin' at this,' he said slowly, stirring his coffee. 'I want ter know who sent you to that bungalow, an' everythin' you know about it.'

' 'Strewth! You're a 'busy'!' The old man half-rose from his chair in his sudden alarm.

'Sit down!' snapped Mr. Budd sharply. 'You're quite right. I'm a busy, an' a very busy busy! Now, come on! Spill the beans. There's one dead man already in this business,' continued the stout superintendent sternly, 'an' there's seven more who may die. If they do, that'll be eight murders — an' you're in it up to the neck.'

'I tell yer I don't know nothin',' whined the old man. 'I was paid ter go an' look after the place, that's all.'

'Who paid yer?' demanded Mr. Budd.

'A feller I met in a pub,' answered Mr.

Hutchin, now reduced to a shivering wreck in his terror. 'I don't know 'is name, an' I don't know nothin' about him; I'd never seen 'im before. He asked me if I'd like ter earn fifty quid, an' when I said I would, 'e told me ter go to that bungalow an' wait until a bloke turned up with a glass dragonfly. I was ter say 'Blue Butterflies' to 'im, an' then clear out. That's all I know. May I never move from this spot if I'm tellin' a lie!'

'An' what about them seven men?' asked Mr. Budd. 'How did they get there?'

'They was there when I got there,' replied the old man. 'I 'ad ter feed 'em every day with a sort o' beef extract — open their mouths an' shove it down their throats — that an' generally look after 'em. It wasn't an 'ard job, though, an' I was paid in advance.'

'I'm surprised this feller trusted you,' grunted Mr. Budd.

'If you'd seen 'im you wouldn't 'ave tried ter do any double-crossin' with 'im,' said Mr. Hutchin earnestly. ' 'E was a queer bloke — sort o' sent cold shivers through yer jest ter look at 'im, it did! He told me if I let 'im down, it 'ud be the end o' me — an' 'e meant it!'

The fat detective swallowed the contents of his coffee cup.

'What about the music from the 'arp?' he said. 'Did yer have ter keep that goin' all the time?'

The old man shook his head.

'Only at night,' he answered. 'I 'ad ter keep it goin' all night. But yer couldn't open the winder without it playin'!'

'An' you was there three weeks,' murmured the big man thoughtfully. 'D'yer know what the meanin' o' 'Blue Butterflies' is?'

'No, I don't knew nothin' more than I've told yer,' declared Mr. Hutchin. 'If I'd thought there was anythin' wrong — '

'Naturally, you couldn't have done!' interrupted Mr. Budd sarcastically. 'There was nothin' ter suggest that to yer, was there? Drink up yer coffee an' come along with me.'

' 'Ere, what are you goin' ter do?' demanded the alarmed Hutchin excitedly.

'I'm detainin' you!' retorted Mr. Budd.

'Your story may be true, an' it may not, an' you're just goin' ter sit quietly in a nice little cell until I've found out!'

Mr. Hutchin argued and pleaded and threatened, but he was escorted to the police station and handed over to a hard-hearted sergeant, who locked him up with great relish and made no effort to disguise the fact.

Having disposed of Mr. Hutchin, the fat man returned to Scotland Yard, where he found Leek awaiting him.

'You don't mean ter say you managed ter wake up?' he said. 'Well, well, wonders 'ull never cease! You'll be sayin' somethin' really intelligent before the day's out if yer go on like this.'

'As a matter o' fact, I've got a theory — ' began the sergeant.

'Tell me about it,' said Mr. Budd, sitting down at his desk and turning over several reports that lay on the blotting pad. 'It's a long time since I had a good laugh!'

'Well,' began the sergeant, 'it's struck me that the I.R.A. may be behind this business — '

'Why not the A.R.P., or the Y.M.C.A.?' snapped Mr. Budd. 'I'll tell yer somethin'. There are three men behind this business — Abel Crossplatt, a feller called Lee Berend, and Mitchell Pettegew — '

'The dead man?' exclaimed the astonished Leek.

'He's not dead!' said Mr. Budd, shaking his head. 'He's very much alive. An' I think 'e'll soon be kickin',' he added softly — 'kickin' like blazes!'

# 9

## Blue Butterflies

The lean sergeant stared at him, his mouth half-open and his eyes wide from sheer amazement.

'Pettegew ain't dead!' he gasped incredulously. 'But 'e was stabbed outside 'is 'ouse in Streatham — '

'I know,' said Mr. Budd calmly; 'but that doesn't make any difference!'

Leek looked at him as though he had taken leave of his senses, which, in truth, for one wild moment, the sergeant thought he had.

'I don't know what yer talkin' about,' he mumbled. 'The man was stabbed, an' he ain't dead? Didn't it kill him, then?'

'Think it out,' said the fat man. 'It'll keep you quiet while I do some work.'

Leek took the hint, and relapsed into a puzzled silence, while Mr. Budd carefully read through the reports and cablegrams on his desk and made a few notes in his big, sprawling writing.

Just before one o'clock he swept the papers together, locked them in a drawer and got ponderously to his feet.

'We'll have a bite o' bread an' cheese,' he announced, 'an' then we'll get off.'

'Off where?' asked Leek curiously.

'To Clacton,' answered Mr. Budd. 'You'd better bring yer butterfly-net; we're goin' chasin' blue butterflies!'

He led the way downstairs and out under the arch into Whitehall. A few yards up the wide thoroughfare on the same side was a small public house, and here the fat man ordered bread and cheese and beer. Leek, who neither drank nor smoked, contented himself with a lime-juice and soda and a ham sandwich.

When they had finished this frugal meal they went back and picked up Mr. Budd's ancient car.

It started to rain just outside London, and when they came into Clacton it was pouring in torrents.

The big man pulled up at the police station and went in, to interview the inspector.

There had been no further developments at the bungalow.

The men had been on duty night and day, but no one had come near the place.

Mr. Budd returned to his car and went in search of the divisional surgeon. He found him at home, and learned that the seven sleepers had been removed from the bungalow without any publicity, and were now housed in a special ward of a local hospital. Two London specialists had come down to see them, and they were undergoing an elaborate treatment.

'There's no doubt about it being sleeping-sickness,' declared the doctor emphatically. 'And there's very little chance of any of them recovering, in my opinion. The usual run of the disease is eight months, and these men have been down with it for nearly three, according to Sir Archibald Binner, who is an authority. We may be able to pull 'em through, but it seems very doubtful.'

He accompanied Mr. Budd to the door.

'Looks as if this weather would get worse instead of better,' he remarked, with a glance at the sky. 'The wind's rising, and I shouldn't be surprised if it wasn't blowing a gale before the night's over.'

They felt the force of the wind when they left the shelter of the town and came out on to the front. It came tearing across the angry sea in great gusts that blew the rain before it in sheets. The heavy breakers boomed on the beach and came hissing over the shingle in a smother of spray.

'It's goin' ter be a nasty night,' murmured Mr. Budd, and the shivering Leek agreed.

On the cliffs where the bungalow stood it was even worse. No shadow now sprawled behind the building, and the big man realised just why the harp had been set in the window. The shadow was useless as a means of identification when there was no sun. Then, and at night, the music of the harp would take its place.

A constable was on duty in the porch, and he saluted when Mr. Budd disclosed who he was and produced his warrant card. The other two men were inside, sitting in the kitchen before a cosy fire.

'Now,' said the stout superintendent, when he had taken off his coat and warmed his hands, 'we'll make a thorough search of this place. I didn't have a chance when I was here before ter do it prop'ly. We're lookin' for anythin' that resembles a blue butterfly — understand?'

It was quite evident from their faces that they did not, although they nodded.

Taking a room at a time, they went methodically through everything it contained, but no trace of a blue butterfly did they find, until they came to the big room with its holland-wrapped furniture, and then it was Leek who made the discovery.

He had uncovered a glass-fronted bookcase and was going through the contents, when his exclamation brought Mr. Budd hastily to his side.

'Is this what you're after?' asked the sergeant, and held out a book.

The fat detective took it and read:

'Blue Butterflies. A Romance. By Marie St. Clare Vincent.'

'I s'pose it is,' grunted Mr. Budd, and

207

tried to open the volume; but it refused to open. He discovered why, when he had made a closer examination. All the pages had been glued together to form an apparently solid block. With his penknife he prised the book apart, and then he saw why.

The centre of the pages had been cut out, making a box-like compartment in the middle of the book, and in this, embedded in cotton wool, was a metal object the shape and size of a pigeon's egg.

Mr. Budd tipped it out into the palm of his hand and eyed it wonderingly. It was perfectly smooth, without a join to be seen anywhere, and it weighed heavily.

'What is it?' asked the curious Leek, frowning.

The big man shook his head.

'I don't know,' he answered. 'Maybe there's somethin' inside, but I'm blest if I can see how you open it.'

He turned it about in his fingers, and then, carrying it over to the window, he peered at it attentively, holding it a few inches from his eyes. After a moment he turned.

'Anybody 'ere understand shorthand?' he asked.

'Yes, sir; I do,' replied one of the policemen instantly.

'Well, take a look at these marks, an' tell me if they mean anythin',' said Mr. Budd. The constable went over to him, and he pointed out several minute scratches near one end of the metal egg.

The policeman examined them, and his lips moved soundlessly.

'There's a message here, sir,' he said at last excitedly.

'I thought there might be,' murmured the big man, nodding. 'What does it say?'

'It says, 'Three feet under the bungalow. Blue Butterfly',' answered the man.

Mr. Budd pursed his thick lips and gently rubbed his chin.

''Three feet under the bungalow. Blue Butterfly', eh?' he repeated. 'H'm! Interestin' an' perculiar! It looks ter me as though we should 'ave ter do a little diggin' before we get to the bottom of this business.'

★   ★   ★

Jill Hope paused with her tea-cup halfway to her lips, put it back in its saucer and, setting cup and saucer down on the table, leaned forward and touched her companion on the arm.

'Don't look round,' she whispered; 'but I'm sure that man who has just come in is the man who engaged me to go to the empty house in Great Oram Street.'

Oliver Frayne stared at her across the small table. They were having tea in the lounge of the Regency Palace, and, as usual, the place was crowded.

'Are you sure?' he asked doubtfully.

She smiled.

'I'm quite certain,' she answered. 'There's nothing very extraordinary about it, is there? I suppose the man must have tea somewhere, so why not here?'

'Has he seen you?' he asked.

'I don't think so,' she replied. 'And, anyway, I don't suppose he'd recognise me. He's only seen me once before, and without a hat.'

Oliver began to glance casually round the big lounge. 'Where's he sitting?' he whispered.

'Just by that pillar — near the girl with the cigarette-trolly,' said Jill. He let his eyes roam slowly in the direction she was looking, and presently he saw the man. He was giving an order to a waitress, and Oliver was able to get a good view of him. He was a very ordinary individual. Thinnish, with mouse-coloured hair and a rather sallow compexion.

'I don't see how you can be so certain,' said Oliver. 'I've seen no end of men like him.'

'It's the way he holds his head,' she explained. 'Slightly on one side, as though he were always listening. I think he's a little deaf. I noticed it when he was talking to me.'

Oliver lit a cigarette, flicked the used match into an ashtray, and blew a thin stream of smoke towards the high roof.

'If that's the fellow, we oughtn't to let him out of our sight,' he murmured thoughtfully. 'That fat chap, Budd, would like to know where to find him.'

The girl's eyes sparkled.

'Let's follow him?' she suggested excitedly; but Oliver was dubious.

'You've been in enough trouble as it is,' he said. 'When I think of last night, and that fire — ' He broke off. 'I'll follow him. I owe him one for mixing you up in this business — '

'You're not going on your own,' declared Jill stubbornly. 'If there's any following to be done, we'll do it together. You're not going to have all the fun!'

His experience warned him that it was quite useless to argue. Once Jill had made up her mind, it was impossible to move her. They finished their tea and paid the bill in readiness, and presently the man rose and made his way to the exit.

It was pouring with rain outside, and their quarry snapped his fingers for a taxi.

'If he's going to do much of that,' muttered Oliver, 'this looks like being an expensive business.'

'Never mind,' said the girl impatiently. 'I've got nearly four pounds of the fiver he gave me. Go on, get a cab, or we shall lose him!'

Oliver got a cab just as the other with the unknown man drove off, and, telling the driver to follow it, jumped in beside Jill.

'Here, you'd better take this.' She thrust some crumpled notes into his hand. 'Don't be silly! Take it! We can probably get it back from the police, if we find out anything.'

Oliver was not so sure about that, but he put the money in his pocket without further argument.

The cab in front ran through Leicester Square to the Mall, and on past Victoria Station to Ebury Street. Turning off into a side street, it stopped eventually before a large stucco-fronted house, and the man got out. Oliver told their driver to go past and stop farther down the road. They were just in time to see the other cab drive off, and the man enter the house.

'What do we do now?' muttered Oliver when he had paid off the cab. 'Ring up Scotland Yard and tell my fat friend where this fellow is to be found?'

'I should think that — ' began Jill, and stopped, clutching his arm. 'Look!' she whispered.

A big, closed car had turned into the

street, and pulled up in front of the house into which the man had gone. From it descended a tall man, muffled in a heavy overcoat, the sight of whom drew a little gasp from the girl.

'The Sin-Eater!' she breathed. 'I'm sure it is.'

Oliver was pretty sure, too. The man was the same height and build as the man who had held him up at the empty soap factory.

He crossed the strip of shiny pavement, mounted the steps and knocked. After a short interval he was admitted, and the door shut behind him.

'We've got 'em both now,' said Oliver. 'You wait here, while I find a telephone-box. We'll have those beauties under lock and key before they know where — '

'They're coming out!' interrupted Jill quickly.

The man in the heavy overcoat had reappeared, followed by the other man. They hurried down the steps and got into the waiting car.

'That's awkward,' muttered Oliver. He looked round as the big car moved away from the kerb, saw a taxi coming towards them, and hailed it. The car sped past them as the cab drew in to the pavement, and Jill jerked the door open.

'Keep behind that car!' said Oliver. 'Don't lose sight of it, whatever you do!'

He sank into the seat beside the girl, and neither of them realised where that chase was to end, or what lay at the finish of it.

# 10

## The Secret of the Bungalow

Sergeant Leek heard Mr. Budd's prognostication with a certain lack of enthusiasm that was visible in his long face.

'It's all very well ter talk about diggin',' he protested; 'but where are yer goin' ter start? This place must cover somethin' like a 'undred feet o' ground, an' you can't take up all the floorin' an' just keep on diggin' until yer come to the right spot — '

'When you've finished yer lecture,' interrupted Mr. Budd, 'we'll get on with it. There's certain to be some sort o' sign ter show where we've got to dig — if we have to do any diggin' at all, which isn't certain.'

The sergeant brightened when he heard this. The prospect of a protracted and laborious digging operation had not been an appealing one.

'We'll 'ave these carpets up,' said the big man, 'an' maybe we'll find somethin'.'

The two policemen set to work with a will, and the carpet in the big room was rolled back. Immediately it became evident that all need for further search was at an end. In the middle of the floor was a neatly painted butterfly with sky-blue wings.

'This is the place,' grunted Mr. Budd, and knelt down with difficulty.

The flooring was well-fitting and new, and the section of it which had been cut to form a large, square trap, fitted so well that it was almost undetectable at first glance. The painted butterfly formed the centre, but although Mr. Budd examined the entire area he could find no means provided for raising the trap. He tried the blade of his penknife, but without success.

'What about a corkscrew?' suggested Leek.

'Have we got a corkscrew?' asked the big man.

'There may be one in the kitchen, sir,'

said one of the policemen. 'I'll go and see.'

He hurried away, and presently returned with a gimlet.

'This'll be better, sir, I think,' he said, handing it to Mr. Budd. 'There's a box of old tools under the dresser.'

'That's the very thin',' said the fat man, and began to screw the gimlet into the wood.

'Now,' he went on after a moment, 'let's see if we can shift it.'

Straightening up, he tugged at the handle of the gimlet, and the square trap rose an inch.

'Slip yer fingers under it,' he gasped, red in the face with his exertions, and the two constables obeyed. The square of flooring was lifted up and laid aside to reveal a section of earth.

'H'm,' said Mr. Budd, staring at it, 'we shall 'ave ter do a bit o' diggin' after all! Is there a spade anywhere about the place?'

There was one in the outhouse, said the constable who had discovered the gimlet, and was dispatched to fetch it.

'Now we'll find out the secret of this

place,' murmured the fat detective, with a note of satisfaction in his voice. 'You can start, Leek. You ain't done anythin' yet.'

The sergeant took the spade reluctantly and began to dig. It was by no means easy work to make an impression on that chalky soil, and after a quarter of an hour he had made little headway.

The constable who followed him got along a trifle quicker, but over an hour had passed before they reached the required three feet. And then the spade struck against something hard.

'Go easy now,' said Mr. Budd warningly. 'We've reached whatever it is that's buried here.'

'Go very easy!' said a voice from the doorway. 'The first man who tries to pull a gun'll never try anything else!'

They spun round. Standing on the threshold was the Sin-Eater, a big automatic in one hand, and beside him stood another man similarly armed. So intent had they been on their work that they had noticed nothing to warn them, and the surprise was complete.

'Mr. Abel Crossplatt, I think,' murmured

Mr. Budd sleepily, and the Sin-Eater started.

'You know my name?' he snapped harshly, and the big man nodded.

'I know quite a lot about yer,' he answered. 'I was readin' an interestin' cable about you this mornin'.'

The Sin-Eater recovered quickly from his surprise.

'Well, it won't do you much good,' he said. 'Go through their pockets, Pettegew. You needn't worry about the two cops. They don't arm the police in this country.'

Leek's jaw dropped when he heard the name. Pettegew! But this man wasn't Pettegew. There was no likeness at all. There must be two Pettegews. This man, and the man who had died. So that's what Budd had meant.

'So you're the feller who should have received them playin' cards,' said Mr. Budd with interest, as the man called Pettegew advanced to carry out the Sin-Eater's order. 'You'll find my gun in me right 'and pocket. My sergeant don't carry firearms. It'd be too risky. We ain't afraid of his shootin' himself, but he might shoot somebody important — '

'Stop talking!' snapped Crossplatt. 'Is that the lot?' he added, as Pettegew came back with Mr. Budd's automatic.

'Yes,' said the man.

'You'd better go and see if you can find some rope, and we'll tie 'em up,' said the Sin-Eater. 'They've saved us a lot of work, but we don't want to stay here longer than we can help.'

Pettegew nodded and went out.

'What did you do with the man on the door?' asked Mr. Budd gently.

'Clubbed him!' said the Sin-Eater briefly. 'How much do you know about this business?'

Mr. Budd yawned.

'Quite a lot,' he answered. 'Not as much as I'm goin' ter know, but quite a lot.' He yawned again, and then suddenly put a question: 'What's happened to Lee Berend?'

Again he succeeded in shocking the Sin-Eater to startled surprise.

'How did you find all this out?' he muttered. 'Berend's dead. It was his death that caused all this trouble — '

'That's a lie!' snarled a fresh voice from the door. 'Drop that pistol, Crossplatt, and don't move! I'd just as soon shoot you in the back as any other way!'

'Melladew!' muttered the Sin-Eater. 'Melladew!'

'That's me!' said the newcomer, coming on out of the shadow of the doorway. 'Drop that pistol — quick, or you'll be as full of 'oles as a piece of wire-netting!'

The automatic fell with a clatter from Crossplatt's hand.

'Kick it towards me!' snapped Melladew. 'And you needn't expect Pettegew to help you. He won't be able to help anyone for a very long time.' He stooped and picked up the pistol, which the Sin-Eater had viciously kicked towards him. 'You dirty, double-crossing rat!' he continued harshly. 'I've got you at last!'

'This place seems ter have become popular all of a sudden,' murmured Mr. Budd sleepily. 'What's brought you here?'

'Crossplatt!' snarled Melladew. 'I've been after him for weeks. It was he and Berend and Pettegew who started all this trouble. The Thieves' Tontine — that's what he called it. There were twelve of us in it, until Andy Shelor was shot by a Federal Agent — '

'What was this Thieves' — what-yer-may-call it?' interrupted the big man.

'It was Crossplatt's idea,' answered Melladew. 'We were to operate for five years. And the proceeds of all our coups was to be banked in a common fund out of which we were to draw a certain sum each week sufficient to live on. At the end of five years the money was to be divided equally between us — if any of us died, their share went to the rest. Work hard for five years and then retire, like any ordinary businessman, with a fat bank balance. Oh, yeah, it was a grand scheme — only Crossplatt didn't mention that he and Berend and Pettegew were the only ones who were going to retire!'

'You damned squeaker!' said the Sin-Eater between his teeth.

'You shut up!' snapped Melladew. 'Your little game's finished, and you'd better keep quiet! I've waited a long time, but I guess I'm coming off best in the end.

There's ten million dollars in that pit, and I'm going to have it!'

'If you'd only be sensible, Melladew,' grunted the Sin-Eater, 'there's no reason why we shouldn't share it — '

'Like we were supposed to do in the first place, eh?' sneered Melladew contemptuously. 'Trying to go back to the original scheme, eh? You're too late, Crossplatt. Don't you wish, now, that you'd inoculated me with some of your sleeping-sickness germs — like the other seven of us? I'll bet you do!'

He chuckled. So that was the explanation of the seven sleepers, thought Mr. Budd. The whole thing was now practically clear. There were only one or two points about which he was doubtful.

'Pick up that spade,' continued Melladew, 'and dig the money out!'

Crossplatt hesitated, but the other made a menacing gesture with his automatic, and, snarling an oath, the Sin-Eater picked up the spade and approached the hole in the floor.

But he never started to dig. With a sudden movement that took Melladew completely by surprise, he flung the spade at him, and almost at the same moment dropped into the shallow pit and crouched down.

Melladew fired as the spade hit him, and the bullet struck a shower of splinters from the edge of the trap. And then, as he went down, the Sin-Eater sprang out of the hole and flung himself upon him.

His evident object was to gain possession of the automatic, but the incident had given the two policemen their opportunity. Before he could wrench the weapon from Melladew's hand they had seized him by the arms and dragged him to his feet.

'Now, you keep still!' growled the bigger of the men. 'We've had enough of you for one evening!'

Crossplatt tried to struggle, but he was like a child in the grip of the two burly men, and, realising that it was useless, gave it up, glowering sullenly between them.

'That's fine!' grunted Mr. Budd, jerking the pistol from Melladew's hand. 'Now the party's more evenly balanced.

Go along an' see how that other feller is, will yer, Leek, an' what's happened to Pettegew? We've got the whole bunch now.'

The lean sergeant obeyed, and Mr. Budd surveyed the Sin-Eater sleepily.

' 'Journeys end in lovers' meetin's',' he quoted softly. 'Not that you'd call this a lovers' meetin', by a long way. I want you, Mr. Abel Crossplatt, an' I want you very badly. You haven't long come out of an American prison, an' now you're goin' into an English one!'

'On what charge?' snarled the Sin-Eater.

'Murder!' snapped the big man laconically. 'There'll be other charges, but that's the important one. The murder of Mitchell Pettegew on the night o' September the tenth — '

'You can't prove it,' muttered Crossplatt, his thin, swarthy face grey.

'I think I can,' murmured Mr. Budd, and before the other realised what he was going to do, he stepped quickly forward, jerked open the man's coat and twitched a wallet out of his breast pocket. His podgy fingers moved rapidly through the contents, and he produced seven playing cards — the original seven cards which poor little Pettegew had shown him in the saloon bar of the Red Lion on the night he had met his death.

'That's proof enough,' he remarked. 'I guessed you'd keep 'em. It won't be long before you have ter find someone to eat your sins for yer, an' I reckon it 'ull be a pretty big mouthful.'

Crossplatt glared at him murderously.

'I wish I'd finished you off — that night in the garden!' he snarled viciously.

Mr. Budd yawned.

'I dare say you do,' he retorted, 'an' there's many more before you who 'ave felt the same.' He looked round at Melladew, who was groaning and rubbing his chest where the heavy spade had struck him. 'There's one or two other thin's I'd like ter know,' he said, 'an' you might as well tell me.'

'I'll tell you anything you like, if it'll help to hang that swine!' said Melladew, with a venomous glance at the Sin-Eater. 'What do you want to know?'

'Not a great deal,' answered the fat

detective. 'I've put two an' two together pretty well, I think. But I'd just like ter fill in the gaps. Who brought this money to England?'

'Berend,' replied Melladew. 'It was in the American Bank of New York, and when Crossplatt decided to double-cross the rest of us he drew it all out and sent Berend with it to England. He had to take Berend and Pettegew into his confidence, because their signatures, as well as his own, were necessary on the cheque.'

'I see,' said Mr. Budd, nodding. 'Berend brought the money over, an' hid it in this bungalow, an' before he could notify Crossplatt where it was, he heard that 'e'd been arrested an' it was too late. How did he hear that?'

'Pettegew cabled him,' answered Melladew promptly. 'He also told him that the rest of us had got on to the game and were on our way to England, which was true. That swine there was in prison — he'd got caught out over a gambling joint and had been sent down for six months — and we couldn't get any satisfaction out of Pettegew. We guessed there was something phoney going on, when we found that Berend had gone, and we followed him — at least, the others did. I stayed in New York to keep an eye on Pettegew. That's how I knew about the cable. I saw him send it, and I managed to get hold of a copy.'

'I see,' said Mr. Budd, nodding.

'You'd've made a good detective!' continued the big man. 'These seven fellers came over and found Berend, an' he decoyed 'em down here somehow an' gave 'em a dose of sleepin'-sickness to keep 'em quiet. Is that right?'

'That's how I figure it out,' said Melladew, nodding. 'He was living at an address in Victoria then. The sleeping-sickness was some stuff of Crossplatt's. He'd used it before.'

'An' then you came over?' prompted the fat man gently.

'I followed Pettegew,' replied the other laconically.

'It's all comin' as clear as daylight,' said Mr. Budd complacently. 'Berend buries the money under this bungalow, which he chooses because o' the perculiar shadow which the sun throws, an' which makes it easy to identify. To make it more easy he puts an aeolian harp in the kitchen window, an' then he sets ter work to leave clues so as Pettegew an' this feller 'ere can find it. That's all clear. What I don't understand is why he went about lettin' 'em know in such a roundabout way, an' how 'e got hold o' that dragonfly.'

'He made it,' said Melladew. 'He'd been a glass-blower once, and he was always pottering about with things like that. As for the reason why he went to such trouble, it was because he was afraid of me — or, rather, afraid that I might discover what he'd done with the money.'

'Surely he could have told Pettegew?' murmured the stout superintendent.

'He was dead before Pettegew arrived in England,' answered Melladew. 'He died in his car on the Colchester road. He'd always suffered with his heart, and this attack finished him. Before he died he managed to scribble a message to Pettegew, whom he knew was arriving the next day, on seven playing cards, which was all he had to write on — he was very fond of playing patience, and always carried a pack about with him — and in his dying state he gave these to a labourer who found him, asking the man to post them separately to Mitchell Pettegew.'

'I see,' said Mr. Budd, nodding quickly, 'an' the man sent them to the wrong Pettegew. I thought somethin' like that must 'ave happened.'

'Pettegew reached England and went to Berend's lodging, where he found the glass dragonfly and learned that Berend was dead,' continued Melladew. 'He didn't know the meaning of the dragonfly, but he thought Crossplatt did, and when Crossplatt was released from prison and came to England he arranged for the red ebony box to come into his possession.'

'But why adopt that elaborate method o' gettin' hold of the girl?' asked Mr. Budd.

'Because he knew Melladew was watching him,' broke in the Sin-Eater harshly. 'Melladew was following him everywhere he went, and he didn't want him to know where I was. He sent me a note to say that the box was at Great Oram Street — '

'By messenger,' interrupted Melladew. 'And I intercepted it and read it before sending it on.'

'An' sent me that card tellin' me about it,' put in the big man softly, 'hopin' that I'd catch Crossplatt when he called. That woul've left yer with only Pettegew to deal with. H'm, yes, it's all clear. I s'pose yer found this labourer feller an' 'e told yer about the cards Berend had asked him ter send? That's how yer got on ter the wrong Pettegew, poor feller! He died because 'is name happened ter be the same. You're goin' ter pay for that, Crossplatt.'

There was a silence, broken by the heavy patter of the rain on the roof and the wild screaming of the wind. The Sin-Eater glared at him malevolently, and from him to Melladew. One of the policemen cleared his throat, and the vapour-lamp flickered. Mr. Budd had turned towards the door, with the intention of calling to Leek, when there came a queer rumbling sound and the floor shook and shivered beneath his feet. The lamp flickered again,

232

and rocked back and forth on the table. The whole building vibrated, as though heavy traffic were passing in its immediate vicinity, and everything in sight seemed to quiver and move.

The fat detective stared in amazement as the ceiling danced above him and the walls swayed, and a violent shock made the bungalow shiver from foundation to roof. And then he realised what was happening.

'For God's sake get out!' he shouted suddenly. 'It's a landslide! We're slipping into the sea!'

There was a rumbling crash that split into a series of thuds as he finished speaking, and the building lurched like a drunken man. The furniture in the room went sliding and tumbling over the floor, and Mr. Budd clutched wildly at a heavy chair to try to keep his balance. But it slid away from his grasp and he cannoned into the two policemen and the Sin-Eater, bringing them down with him. The lamp overturned and went out, and in the pitch darkness he heard somebody scream. And then a rain of plaster and broken wood poured down upon him, and straining and groaning like a storm-racked ship, the bungalow subsided with the crumbling cliff, and slid rapidly and noisily down towards the sea.

# 11

## The End Of It All

Mr. Budd only had very vague recollections of what happened during the ensuing few minutes. He seemed to become the centre of a chaotic whirlpool of noise, and, partially stunned, was flung this way and that until his head swam.

The air was full of falling debris that crashed and pattered round him in a never-ceasing cascade, with which was mingled the shivering splintering of breaking glass. The slithering, swaying motion continued for what seemed to him an eternity before, with a shattering shock that knocked what little breath he had left out of him, the remains of the bungalow struck the beach. For a minute or two there was a thunderous volley of earth and stones that beat on the walls and roof, but gradually this subsided to a pattering no louder than the rain, and

235

then died away altogether, until there was no other sound but the roar of the sea and the howling of the gale.

Breathless, bruised, and thoroughly shaken, the big man crawled out from the wreckage of broken furniture that had fallen about him, and drew out his torch.

As the white beam dispersed the darkness and went roving about the room, he gasped as he saw the destruction that the landslide had caused. There were great cracks in the walls and in the ceiling; the window was gone completely, glass and frame; the door had been wrenched off its hinges. A pile of broken furniture lay heaped in one corner, and the floor had been ripped up, so that the planks which had formed it stuck out at all angles.

It was a miracle, thought Mr. Budd, that anyone should have survived such an appalling catastrophe, and concluded that it was due to the fact that the bungalow was built mostly of wood. Had it been a brick building it would have completely collapsed and buried them in the ruins.

Unsteadily he got to his feet and looked

to see what had happened to the others. The two policemen were unconscious, pinned under a heavy table. The Sin-Eater was dead. A beam from the roof had crushed his head, and the fat detective turned quickly away from the unpleasant sight.

Of Melladew there was no sign at all, and he was puzzled to know what could have happened to the man, until he remembered the gaping hole in the floor where the trap had been, and concluded that he must have fallen through this during the descent.

Going over to the two constables, he pulled the table away with difficulty, and examined them. As far as he could judge they were only stunned.

A groan from the doorway made him turn, and he saw the lean figure of Leek stagger across the threshold. The sergeant's long face was streaked with blood, and he looked dazed and bewildered.

'What 'appened?' he mumbled. 'I was just comin' back 'ere, when the whole place started shakin' an' rockin' an' down we went! What 'appened?'

'A landslide,' answered Mr. Budd

shakily. 'All this rain, I s'pose. Are you hurt?'

'I don't think I am,' replied the sergeant, a little vaguely. 'Me 'ead hurts a bit.'

'Let's have a look at you,' said the big man. He peered at Leek's wounds, and nodded.

'You're all right,' he said. 'You've got a bit of a cut on yer head, an' a nasty bump over yer eye, but you'll live! What happened ter Pettegew and that other feller?'

'Pettegew's out there,' answered Leek, jerking his thumb at the doorway. 'I don't know what 'appened to the constable — he was outside — '

'We'll go outside,' interrupted Mr. Budd, 'an' see what the damage is like.'

He made his way up the sloping floor to the doorway and out into the hall. The wreckage here was even greater than in the room he had left. Broken glass and splintered wood lay everywhere, and the front door had been forced through the roof. Water was frothing angrily round the ruins of the step; the boom of the breakers sounded unpleasantly close.

A tornado of wind and rain greeted them as they forced their way out, and they were nearly blown off their feet. They clung on to the broken side of the bungalow, however, and worked their way round, until they faced the cliff.

Mr. Budd flashed on his torch, and a startling sight met his eyes. Where the bungalow had been a great hole gaped, from which a steep slope of earth and chalk led down to the beach. A slice of the cliff had subsided.

'You stop 'ere an' keep an eye on Pettegew, an' them policemen,' said the big man, shouting to make himself heard above the roar of the sea, and the noise of the wind. 'I'm goin' up that slope.'

He began to climb the unstable mound towards the cliff top, the rain hissing and splashing around him, and the wind tearing at his clothes. Halfway to the top he came upon Melladew. The man had a great gash across his temple, which was bleeding badly, but he was alive.

Mr. Budd took out his handkerchief, improvised a bandage, and then continued his climb. As he staggered, panting,

239

muddy, and wet to the skin, on to the top of the cliff, he heard shouts, and saw lights approaching. A little army of men came hurrying towards him, and to his surprise he saw among them Oliver Frayne and Jill Hope.

'Where's the bungalow?' asked the astonished young man as he recognised Mr. Budd.

'Down there!' gasped the fat detective, jerking his head towards the edge of the cliff. ' 'Ow did you get here?'

'We followed the Sin-Eater and another man,' answered the girl. 'We saw what happened, and we went to fetch the police.'

'That's right, sir,' put in a voice, and Mr. Budd saw it was the inspector from Clacton who spoke. 'You've been having some trouble here?'

'Oh, no!' said Mr. Budd, who was both tired and irritable. 'We've 'ad an argument with a bunch o' crooks, an' a minor earthquake, that's all. Nothin' that you could call trouble! You'd better get busy. There's a man halfway down that slope who's seriously wounded, an' two of your fellers are knocked out. There's another somewhere, but I haven't found him.'

The inspector was a little resentful over the big man's sarcasm, but he was a capable man, and calling his small force together, began issuing orders.

Lights twinkled along the cliff top and down the slope. The third constable was found lying on a ledge of the cliff, and he was in such a serious condition that he was rushed off, with Melladew, to hospital in the car that had brought the Divisional-Inspector. The body of the Sin-Eater was brought up and laid on the wet grass, covered with one of the policemen's capes, to await the ambulance, which the men who had gone into Clacton had been instructed to send back.

Mr. Budd, seated on the running-board of one of the cars, a damp and unlighted cigar clenched between his teeth, watched the scene of activity wearily.

Mitchell Pettegew and the two police-men, who had recovered their senses, had just been brought up, when the inspector came over to the fat detective.

'There are two large steel boxes

half-buried in the earth down there,' he said. 'D'you know what they contain?'

'Ten million dollars,' answered Mr. Budd, and Jill Hope gasped.

'Ten million dollars,' echoed the astonished inspector. 'Are you joking — '

'There's nothin' funny about that money,' broke in the big man seriously. 'Every dollar's stained red with somebody's blood.'

During the three days that followed the destruction of the bungalow, and the death of the Sin-Eater, Mr. Budd was a very busy man indeed.

There was much to be done before he could finally say that the case was completed.

Pettegew, after being treated for his wound at the hospital in Clacton, had been formally charged with being an accessory to the murder of his namesake, and after appearing before the magistrate, had been committed for trial. There was nothing very much against Melladew, and he was detained as a witness. On his information, Mr. Budd succeeded in finding the labourer who had discovered the dying Berend, and getting his sworn statement, and this contained a description of a man who had previously questioned him, and which was recognisable as that of Abel Crossplatt.

On the afternoon of the third day, the fat man came back to his office after making his last report to the Assistant Commissioner, and sank wearily into his chair.

'That's that,' he grunted. 'It's all over now bar the trial, an' that should be plain sailin'. I don't think I ever remember a queerer business, though.'

'What's goin' ter happen to the money?' asked Leek.

'The Home Office an' the American Embassy are dealin' with that,' answered Mr. Budd, lighting one of his cigars with great relish. 'It'll go to America, I s'pose. It was stolen there, or the equiv'lent was, by this Sin-Eater feller an' his bunch.'

'Why did 'e call himself the Sin-Eater?' inquired the sergeant curiously.

'He followed that trade at one time, if yer can call it a trade,' replied his superior, blowing out a cloud of smoke contentedly. 'That's how I first got on to him. I put an inquiry out, an' got a reply from the New York Police Bureau, tellin' me all about Crossplatt, an' his friends. The police over there knew all about 'em, but they'd never been able ter get anythin' on 'em.'

'What's goin' to 'appen to those seven fellers with sleepin' sickness?' said Leek, after a pause. 'Is there any chance of 'em gettin' better?'

'Not much, accordin' ter the doctor,' said Mr. Budd, shaking his head. 'Maybe it'll be better for them if they don't. This business has blown their graft wide open, an' they'd prob'ly be extradited ter answer charges against 'em in the States.'

There was a tap on the door, and a messenger entered. He laid a slip of paper in front of Mr. Budd, and waited. The big man looked at it, yawned and raised his sleepy eyes to the man.

'Bring the feller up,' he said, with a sigh.

'Who is it?' asked Leek, as the messenger departed.

'Young Frayne,' murmured Mr. Budd. 'I don't know what he wants. Maybe he's lost that girl of his again.'

But that was not the reason for Oliver's visit. He came cheerfully into the office, and smiled a greeting.

'Jill and I are getting married,' he announced, without preliminary. 'We've fixed a good job, and we've decided not to wait any longer. I've come to give you a formal invitation to the wedding.'

The fat man looked at him through a cloud of acrid smoke.

'I'm very glad to 'ear it,' he said, 'but I'm not used ter weddin's. I tell yer what I will do, though. I'll give yer a weddin' present, as soon as this trial's over.'

'Not that ten million dollars?' said Oliver, his eyes twinkling, and Mr. Budd shook his head.

'No,' he answered. 'I'll give yer the glass dragonfly. It'll be useful, maybe, when yer tell the story to your grandchildren!'

## THE END

We do hope that you have enjoyed reading this large print book.

Did you know that all of our titles are available for purchase?

We publish a wide range of high quality large print books including:
**Romances, Mysteries, Classics**
**General Fiction**
**Non Fiction and Westerns**

Special interest titles available in large print are:
**The Little Oxford Dictionary**
**Music Book, Song Book**
**Hymn Book, Service Book**

Also available from us courtesy of Oxford University Press:
**Young Readers' Dictionary**
**(large print edition)**
**Young Readers' Thesaurus**
**(large print edition)**

For further information or a free brochure, please contact us at:
**Ulverscroft Large Print Books Ltd.,**
**The Green, Bradgate Road, Anstey,**
**Leicester, LE7 7FU, England.**
**Tel:** (00 44) 0116 236 4325
**Fax:** (00 44) 0116 234 0205

*Other titles in the*
*Linford Mystery Library:*

# SERPENT'S TOOTH

## Michael R. Collings

Eric Johansson lives in Fox Creek with his elderly grandmother. But young Carver Ellis discovers him dead in his bed, having been severely beaten. Then, unfortunately for Ellis, the police officer arrives on the scene already convinced that Ellis murdered the victim. Victoria Sears, and her friend down-mountain, Lynn Hanson, work with Deputy Richard Wroten to clear Ellis and uncover why Johansson died. Can they do it before a crucial piece of evidence disappears?

# BLACKOUT!

## Steve Hayes and David Whitehead

When Diana Callan was beaten to death, all the evidence suggested that her husband, former Green Beret Christopher Callan, was the killer. He had returned from Afghanistan and developed violent blackouts, during which he could remember nothing. But another suspect was in the frame and if Chris could provide enough evidence to prove his innocence the real murderer could be punished. However, that was easier said than done . . . especially while Chris was involved with the girlfriend of a psychotic hoodlum.

# THE KILL DOG

## John Burke

Maggie is in Prague on a Market Research project. But when a Russian tank rolls up outside her hotel, dashing all her plans, she decides to face the country's menacing and violent situation and drive towards the border. On the way, she acquires a passenger — a fugitive. Jan is a Czech archaeologist, carrying a valuable secret, ignorant of its significance or value. But when he eventually faces his enemies in Czechoslovakia, events prove more dramatic than he'd ever anticipated.

# THE ENIGMAS OF HUGO LACKLAN

## John Light

In *The Enigmas of Hugo Lacklan*, Alexander Dunkley relates some of the puzzling anecdotes of his social anthropologist friend. Though quite unacademic, these questions, and others, intrigue Hugo. In *The Vanishing Punk*, how did the punk thief vanish after his crimes? And we can only wonder what the reason was for the odd behaviour of the *Five Elderly Gentlemen*. Then, in *The Expensive Daub*, why were hideous daubs selling for such high prices from a London gallery?